WHERE THE WILD BLUEBERRIES GROW

DARYL N. PATTERSON

CABIN
BOOKS

CABIN BOOKS
CHICO, CA.

Published by Cabin Books
Chico, California 95973
Printed in the United States of America

Additional copies of this book may be obtained from Cabin Books

EAN-13   978-0-9646761-4-5

Library of Congress Catalog Card Number: 2019918032

First Printing: April 2020

cabinbookspublishing@gmail.com

To my Family, May Life Always be an Adventure

MORE THAN LEGEND

INDIAN SKY

THE GREAT RIFT

TABLE OF CONTENTS

WHERE THE WILD BLUEBERRIES GROW

1

WHERE THE
WILD BLUEBERRIES GROW

For Sarah, the mystery of an old family letter was the first link of what would be a chain of events that would completely change her life, but in a way you would not expect. The letter talked about a small fleet of treasure-laden ships that had become storm damaged and eventually buried in place. She always enjoyed a good mystery, but this one had the appearance of being unsolvable. However, what Sarah finds in the days to come would be surprising even to her.

It took the ravage of a hurricane to remind locals that there was still an unsolved mystery in their backyard. Numerous old shipwrecks were reappearing along many of the waterways. Cleanup after hurricane "Earl" was beginning to wind down after about three weeks of mayhem. Things were gradually getting back to more of a normal routine and daily life.

It was a typical moody day along the South Carolina Coast with the fog drifting in and ocean waves crashing and racing up the beach in among the Palmetto palm trees waving to and fro in the early morning breeze.

Mist drifted over the numerous river channels and sprawling wetlands. How strangely captivating was the sound of the loon as it echoed across the marshes and through the trees draped in

Spanish moss.

It was a pleasant time for Sarah to be out walking, admiring the woods and thinking about her own life and where it was going. Things in general had not gone well for her as regards relationships with the opposite sex and with people overall. It seemed that throughout high school and now in college her path was following a more and more divergent course distancing herself from her acquaintances. Sarah was not sure what that path was, but she enjoyed history and all things botanical. And so it was that day she was off to a patch of wild blueberries quite some distance away in the woods.

Her younger sister, Sadie, accompanied her that day as she had numerous times before. For the most part she didn't mind, but due to Sarah's infrequent spells of dizziness that rendered her immobile at times, she gladly tagged along to make sure she was safe.

But today was going to be different she told herself. The sun sparkled through the leaves softly lighting the forest floor. A colorful Carolina Wren sang from a nearby tree and flowering Golden Rod lined the meandering pathway. The patch of blueberries that Sarah had spotted a few days before was a good half mile away. Crossing over a small creek and a seldom used dirt road brought them into a meadow and a large undeveloped tract of land.

"Wow! Look at all the blueberries. This berry patch is immense," realized Sadie as they traversed across the open field.

"It is," agreed her sister. "But what's interesting these blueberries appear to be of a different variety than the norm," she replied stooping down to examine them more closely.

"Blueberries are blueberries, let's start picking," insisted Sadie.

"Is that a challenge that I'm hearing?" asked Sarah raising her voice.

"Yes! Why not. Blueberries are not a quick pick, but they are sure good," replied Sadie.

2

While picking, Sarah kept looking at the trees just beyond the berry patch. What a tangled landscape. She could make out sprawling Southern live oaks mixed with maples draped in Spanish moss, as well as Wax myrtle trees forming an impenetrable thicket in places. The trumpet creeper vine was also present wrapping itself around the tree trunks like snakes making trespass into the dark forest ever so foreboding.

It seemed like an eternity for her to work around to the opposite side of the berry bushes. Feeling a bit tired she plunked down on a large tree root and invited Sadie over to join her.

"Look, almost two pails," she boasted.

"Good work, Sadie," complemented Sarah. "Sit down and rest up a bit."

"Have you noticed how mom has been depressed of late," spoke up her younger sister.

"Well, yes. Besides the divorce with dad, there's the issue with the insurance company. It appears they're not going to fully pay for the tree damage we sustained during the storm. I need to get a part time job to see us through," Sarah answered after a pause.

"You could get your old job back at the drive-in," joked Sadie.

"Oh please," protested Sarah. That was terrible. Every guy in town was trying to hit on me."

"But you were so cute in that mini-skirt," teased her sister.

"Sadie, you are no help. Perhaps though, since you are such a proficient berry picker you could come out on weekends and earn some extra cash," countered Sarah.

"I would probably eat half of the profits even before I got home," laughed Sadie.

"What's that under your foot?" asked her sister.

"Under my foot?" questioned Sadie lifting one foot and then the other.

"Something grey," observed Sarah.

"Stepping stone maybe," Sadie guessed scraping her shoe across the top of it.

3

Using a large stick Sarah scraped away the dirt revealing a large rectangular stepping stone. It had a greyish-blue cast and had some strange markings on it.

"That's interesting, commented Sadie.

"If there's one, maybe there's more, and where do they lead?" wondered Sarah.

"Sister, you have that look in your eyes. It's another mystery!" declared Sadie.

"Probably short-lived," laughed Sarah.

"Look, over there," pointed Sadie. "Another one, but it has been broken by those huge roots."

"These are quarried stones, probably blue granite, not concrete," realized her older sister, "Which makes them very old."

"Where do they lead?" questioned Sadie.

Looking back to the first stone their eyes swung around in the suspected path.

"Wow!" commented Sarah, "this is incredible."

"Look at the size of the trees back in there," observed Sadie.

"I wonder if there is anything in there," contemplated Sarah.

"Kinda dangerous if you ask me," responded her sister.

"Can't be too dangerous, they are just trees, right?" reasoned Sarah.

"I don't know, those are mighty small spaces to be squeezing through," observed Sadie.

"It is getting a bit late to go poking around," realized Sarah looking at her watch. "Besides we should get those berries back before you eat them all."

"Well, maybe we can come back and investigate a little further. I'm a little curious too," expressed Sadie.

That evening Sarah was curious enough to make a couple of phone calls asking if anyone knew who owned that property. But after making a number of inquiries no one seemed to know, not even the older residents.

While reading in the local newspaper, her mother mentioned there had been a discovery of an old shipwreck that had been exposed along the Waccamaw River. Reading the article herself she found that the recent hurricane and storm surge had uncovered the remains of an unknown ship in its northerly embankment near Tucker's Grove. Treasure hunters and enthusiasts were out in force searching the other waterways for more relics. She thought to herself there were shipwrecks everywhere in the navigable rivers nearby; and didn't give it too much more consideration.

Next day, circumstances didn't allow them to return to the berry patch and explore further. Matter of fact it was quite a disturbing day for Sarah and the rest of the family. Her estranged father was causing them much grief over the final distribution of certain assets after the divorce settlement.

They were a typical happy family a couple of years before, but her parents began drifting apart. Her father quickly married a younger woman which was quite disturbing to her. It was a classic example of complete betrayal, leaving her to deal with a great deal of anger. Sadie and her mom were dealing with it in similar ways and even with a feeling of guilt at times.

Sarah was determined not to let this drag her down. Next day she was ready to focus on something positive, namely her and Sadie's new mystery over at the blueberry patch. Sadie was still moody the next day and was not a happy camper, but was willing to go.

Dressed in their grubbies they headed out mid-morning on a fictitious trip to gather more blueberries. Sarah had the bright idea of bringing along a ball of twine to facilitate their attempt to find their way in and back out of the dense vegetation. By the time they had arrived the fog had completely receded giving better illumination into the dark reaches of the dense forest. Resting for a few minutes they noticed how quiet it was except for an occasional bird call.

"Look, there's a deer watching us," pointed out Sadie near the tree line.

"Hope he's the only one," commented her sister.

"Are you ready?" anxiously spoke up Sadie.

"Yes, I believe so," replied Sarah dusting off her bottom. "Let's tie our pails to this branch back here," she suggested. "And use them as an anchor point for our search line."

"Almost like searching a cave using a string line," compared her sister.

"Indeed so," agreed Sarah who unwound ten to fifteen feet of twine.

"It's going to be hard to keep on a straight line as we dodge back and forth," realized Sadie.

"Problem is we really don't know if there are any more stones, or what alignment they were put in. Hopefully, we can just find one after the other," responded Sarah.

"Okay, you first," urged Sadie.

Slowly Sarah made her way in, swinging over a large drooping limb and then crawling under the next. Sadie was right behind her. About thirty feet in they located another stepping stone, undisturbed.

Suddenly, there was a distant noise that caused them to turn around.

"Did you hear that?" questioned Sadie.

"I did," confirmed her sister repositioning herself to see out beyond the berry patch. "Look, someone is way out by the dirt road."

"Yeah, and whoever it is appears to be looking at a map," observed Sadie. "He, that is I think it is a he, has picked up a pair of binoculars and is now looking up and down the meadow."

Both watched as the person who appeared to be quite tall continued to look in all directions, but mostly toward their location. Suddenly, the individual started violently sneezing and abruptly left; walking toward the old dirt road.

"That was strange," remarked Sadie. "That obviously was a man, but I wonder if someone tipped him off that we were out here."

"I don't know," slowly responded her sister. "But I think we'll be okay."

"Hope so," replied Sadie.

"Whoever it was must be allergic to the ragweed he was standing in," commented Sarah.

Proceeding further through the trees and vines, it seemed to be getting darker as they proceeded.

"There is something just ahead. It almost looks like a wall or something," believed Sarah.

Just as quickly as she said that, her footing gave way and down she fell into a hole that was between two large vines that were hidden under a layer of leaves. The breath was knocked out of her as she landed several feet below in darkness.

"Are you okay?" cried out Sadie in a panic.

"Oh my! That was a fall. I think I'm still in one piece," Sarah finally responded after a long silence.

"Check again. Can you move?" asked her sister.

"Yes, I'm still mobile," she answered. "Nothing broken, but I am scraped up pretty bad in a couple places. My pant leg is torn and I have a painful cut on the side of my left leg. It's very dark down here and all I can see is dim light coming through where I fell in."

"Is there any way to climb out?" next asked Sadie.

"I'm not seeing a way. The bottom is rock and the walls feel like they are all rock-lined as well. There's probably some ugly looking spiders down here as well."

"I could help pull you out if you could climb up to just below the opening," stated Sadie.

"That I don't think I can do," replied Sarah. "There isn't anything to grab hold of."

"I'll have to go out and see if I can get help," concluded Sadie.

"Oh! I'm so mad at myself for this!" exclaimed Sarah.

"Things happen," replied her sister. "I'll be right back."

After a few minutes she heard Sadie calling for help out some distance from the berry patch. She worried about her sister attracting the wrong kind of help.

THE SURVEYOR

Jim Hollingsworth paused to catch his breath after clearing brush along a survey line. Looking back he checked to see if he had a clear line of sight.

Following in his father's footsteps, Jim joined him in his land surveying business which was doing quite well. The only problem was that his dad's health had turned for the worse, putting most of the load on him to run the business, Frankly, he wasn't so much worried about that, but more about his father's condition.

Out of the blue he heard someone calling for help. It came from somewhere further back in the woods. His chainman, Billy Montana was nowhere to be seen. With machete still in hand he hurriedly made his way through the trees down a gradual slope. Pausing he listened again and altered his direction. After a minute, Jim broke out into a clearing and spotted a young blonde-haired teenage girl seemingly in distress.

"Hello! You were calling for help?" he asked hurriedly.

"Yes," she answered slowly. "Sarah! There's a man here with a big sword," she warned.

"It's okay, it's only for cutting brush. Do you need help or not?" demanded Jim.

"Yes, my sister is back in there and she fell into a hole or something," pointed Sadie.

Sarah heard her sister say something about a man with a big sword. She felt panic. What had she gotten them into? A spell of dizziness was trying to overtake her, but she fought it back.

"How old is your sister?" Jim asked as he began wiggling his way between the trunks and the vines in the direction that was indicated.

"She's nineteen, and her name is Sarah," informed Sadie. "Follow the twine," she added.

"Sarah! Can you hear me?" he called out.

"Yes, and who is it that's asking?" she demanded.

"My name is Jim Hollingsworth and I'm a land surveyor who just happened to be working nearby, when I heard a call for help," he informed.

"Oh, good. I thought for a moment you were some deranged murderer or something," Sarah replied in relief.

"Ha! No, nothing like that," commented Jim.

"How did you get back in here? This is one tangled mess." After a pause he continued, "I can't get through here. I'll try more to the left."

Jim slid between two large limbs and crawled for a few feet before standing back up. "Sarah, talk to me," he requested.

"I'm down here," she called out. "I may have fallen into a cellar or a well."

Jim stepped his way over a bundle of vines to arrive at the edge of the hole where Sarah had fallen. Drooping tree limbs and large vines were spider-webbed across the top of the opening.

"This certainly was a booby-trap," realized Jim kneeling down on the edge of the hole still not able to see her yet. "Hello, Sarah, are you injured in any way?"

"No, nothing serious, just a few scrapes and a cut on my leg," she answered. "And Hi! Did you say your name was Jim?" Sarah asked with her voice echoing slightly.

"Yes, it is. This is not going to be easy to get you out," he concluded.

"Do you need to call the Fire Department?" she asked.

"No, I think we can get you out without all that notoriety," stated Jim.

"Thanks, this is embarrassing enough. Did you say we?" asked Sarah.

Yeah, my assistant Billy; he's close by. I'll go back over, get him, and bring my chainsaw. We'll have you out in a jiffy," he encouraged. In a little spot of dim sunlight he got a glimpse of the young woman who was blonde-haired just like her sister. "I'll be back in about fifteen minutes," estimated Jim as he stood back up.

"Okay, but let my sister know so she won't be so worried," she requested.

"Will do."

Jim made his way back out and was able to put Sadie's mind at ease that a rescue was imminent. Returning to the adjacent property he found Billy and explained the situation to him. Billy had wondered what had happened to him in the meantime. After checking the fuel and oil in the chainsaw they were off.

As they approached, Sadie was sitting down and looking particularly glum. Jim introduced Sadie and Billy, and outlined his plan using the chainsaw.

Billy followed Jim as he led the way into the dense vegetation. Once back at the site, Jim instructed Sarah to stand back as far possible while he cut a large limb and a couple of vines. He also suggested that she place her hands over her ears because of the intense noise that would be produced by the gas engine.

Billy assisted as he made the cuts. Chips flew everywhere. Jim cut one thick tree branch about ten feet long. Billy questioned him on what he was planning?

"We're going to make a ladder," he informed after shutting off the saw.

"A stroke of genius," replied Billy.

Firing the saw back up he de-limbed the large branch so that about eight inch stubs were left to serve as hand and footholds.

Finishing the makeshift ladder they placed it in the hole which seemed to be about eight feet deep.

"Sarah, if you are able, go ahead and climb on out," instructed Jim.

"Okay, here goes," she replied.

Sarah quickly came right up and Billy assisted her to step out on the ground. The first thing to catch Jim's attention was her stunning blue eyes.

"Thank you both," she stated regaining her composure.

"Let's carefully work our way back out," suggested Jim.

For the first time she could see what Jim looked like. A dark-haired young man whose age she guessed was a couple years older than she was. He wore a vest like a surveyor would wear, confirming his story. After meeting Billy she was convinced that everything was okay.

"Sarah, except for the cut on your leg are you injured in any other way?" asked Jim.

"No, I'm fine, and I'm really sorry for disturbing you two. You can get back to work now," bluntly stated Sarah, wide-eyed and expressive.

Jim's eyebrows arched. He glanced at Billy and Sadie.

"Sarah!" protested Sadie.

It was her attempt to get her sister to show some degree of thankfulness and not be so rude. A long silence ensued.

"That's a bad cut," pointed out Jim. "I have a first aid kit up at the truck. I would be glad to go get it."

"No need," she shot back.

"Could we at least give you a lift back home?" finally asked Billy who was also concerned about her.

She couldn't hide the fact that it was a severe cut and had bled some.

"No, we can walk back home, it's not that far," replied Sarah.

"Very well, we'll be on our way, but if you still need our help, we'll be just up through those trees," pointed Jim. "May I ask though what you were doing back in there?" he asked.

11

"I rather not say," she replied.

"We were supposed to be picking blueberries," remarked Sadie.

"Okay, just please be more careful," finalized Jim as they headed back to their worksite.

"That was just plain rude what you said to him. After all they did rescue you," stated Sadie.

"Yeah, I know. It's just during times like this they pretend to be nice to you and later on they get under your skin. If you know what I mean," replied her sister.

"I think you're jumping to the wrong conclusion. I think Jim and Billy were genuinely concerned about you," believed Sadie.

Sarah did not reply to this matter any further. But kept thinking about what she had seen just beyond where she had fallen into the hole. There was stonework. What was it? It kept bugging her. She loved a mystery.

Sarah realized she couldn't discuss it with her sister. Sadie would prevent her from doing any further exploration. If there was to be something further she would have to do it on her own.

Jim thought about the slender blonde-haired girl he just rescued and her sudden change of attitude. He wondered what kind of burr was under her saddle. Shaking his head he just shook it off and refocused on the task at hand.

Two days later between classes and other duties, Sarah drove out to park along the dirt road near where she had the accident. There was a bit of intimidation in returning to this place. How should she refer to this place? Time would tell she told herself.

Maneuvering her way back into the trees she kept muttering to herself: "Watch where you step." Sarah gave the hole she had fallen into a wide berth. Beyond that point she came to a wall of vines and rock. It was definitely a stone wall. No doubt hand-fitted. Working around more to her left the aged stonework turned at right angles. Sarah believed this to be a building of some kind. Further investigation showed this to be true. The stone structure apparently was not that large. Like a cabin. The entryway was sealed off by layers of vines and thick shrubbery. How exciting this discovery. How old was this place?

There was nothing further that was visible. It was time to carefully work her way back out. Navigating all the obstacles she was soon standing back out in the clear facing the dense forest that enclosed the stone cabin.

Feelings welled up inside her as she wondered what this place was, who built it, and what had happened here. Sarah was determined to find out more.

"Stone Cabin," she announced. "This is what I shall call it."

Walking back to the car Sarah contemplated that the next step would have to be to find out who owned the property. That information should be available at the Georgetown Courthouse. Maybe tomorrow she thought. It was her turn to cook that night and there was homework to complete.

Georgetown was a small Southern town that had not lost its charm and its historical fascination. Crepe Myrtle and magnolia trees lined many of the town's streets. Small cottages were mixed with large two story colonial homes. Many of the buildings in the business district were constructed in the Planation architectural style, since the county's history was solidly fixed in the Plantation Era. Such was the case with the county buildings found on Screven Street in downtown Georgetown.

Sarah got out of her car and stepped up on the sidewalk. Turning around she almost bumped into a man coming around the corner who wasn't watching either.

"Oh, you scared me!" exclaimed Sarah.

"Sorry," he replied.

Almost simultaneously they recognized each other. They both laughed.

"Sarah!" recognized Jim Hollingsworth.

"You, the surveyor," she responded.

"Yes, and I hope you have been staying out of that berry patch," he stated.

"Well—," she hesitated, not knowing how to answer.

"Ah ha, young lady, you have gone back out there! I'm not going to be out there too many more days to rescue you again," he stated.

"Well excuse me! I will not need any of your further assistance, okay?" answered Sarah getting a little perturbed.

Suddenly she felt faint and unsteady. "Let me hold on to you for a moment," she requested grasping his arm. "I get these dizzy spells from time to time."

"I probably got you all riled up," realized Jim. "Should I take you to a doctor's office?"

"No, no one has been able to find out why I have these spells," confided Sarah. She took a deep breath. "I feel better now." Releasing her grip, she straightened up. "You better get back to work; and I have an errand to run."

"If you're sure you'll be okay?" he questioned.

"Yes, I am," she replied taking another deep breath. "Go, I'm fine," she said waving him off.

"Hope so," said Jim slowly walking and looking back.

Sarah noticed all the rolled up maps he was carrying as he continued down the sidewalk. Turning she headed for the Assessor's Office that was in the adjacent building complex.

The Assessor's plats made no sense to her. She found the right book and page, but it was impossible for her to distinguish what property was what. There were references to Records of Surveys, but these were referenced to monuments and physical features she was not familiar with. Disappointment came over her. What next?

3

THE HIATUS

Could she ask Jim Hollingsworth? She had been rather rude to him; even telling him that she didn't need his help anymore. Basically, telling him to get lost. She really didn't want to involve anyone else. However he did seem pleasant. He was a surveyor and would know how to find out the ownership of that particular property.

He must have an office somewhere. All surveyors have offices, right? She told herself. Looking in the phone book under Land Surveyors, Sarah quickly found Hollingsworth Land Surveying, the phone number, and the office location. She decided to go down there first thing in the morning before he had a chance to leave for the field.

And so it was, Sarah, without telling anyone what she was up to, drove into town the next morning to park in front of his office. She was mentally prepared to apologize to him first. Sarah sat there for a moment thinking about that. Frankly, she didn't like the way she had been behaving. That wasn't her.

"Okay, let's do this," Sarah told herself.

Getting out she proceeded up to the glass door with all the business information on it and opened it. The small waiting room was well lit. Three chairs were lined up on the right side with a customer counter on the left. Sarah approached the counter and spotted a dark-haired woman sitting behind a desk typing away.

"Good morning," spoke up Sarah smiling.

"Well, good morning to you too," she responded getting up. Taking off her glasses she came over to the counter. "How can I help you?"

"I would like to see Jim Hollingsworth about locating the owner of a certain piece of property," explained Sarah.

"You have met Jim, before?" she asked.

"Yes, we've bumped into each other a couple of times. I'm Sarah by the way."

"Glad to meet you. I'm Beth," replied the secretary. "Let me see if Jim is available. Hang on for a minute while I check."

"Thank you," replied Sarah.

Looking around the waiting room she spotted numerous framed plaques and awards for business professionalism. Sarah could hear talking somewhere in the back. She heard the secretary say, "There's a pretty girl here to see you ..." After a moment Beth returned and escorted her through a doorway into the back. Sarah noticed all the drafting tables and numerous map cases as she walked through. She also noticed a draftsman seated at a computer station working on a digital drawing. Apparently Jim had a small office in the rear of the building.

"Just sit here in this chair until he gets off the phone. He'll be right with you," informed Beth in a subdued voice.

Jim was sitting in a swivel chair talking on the phone to someone about how he was a man down and did not know when he could start the job. After he finished talking, Jim swung around to face her and smiled.

"Sarah!" exclaimed Jim. "What a surprise. How can I help you?"

Well, first of all I want to apologize for being somewhat rude the other day," she started off. "I don't mean to be, but ever since my parents have gone through a divorce I have not been in the best of moods."

"Sorry to hear that," he commented.

16

"On another note, I need you to help me find the owner of the property where you rescued me," she continued.

"Why? Are you going to sue them or something?" asked Jim concernedly.

"No, no, I'm just curious to find out, that's all," answered Sarah.

"Since I'm working next door, I may already have some information on that subject. But I'll have to check and see. The best thing would be for you to call me tomorrow about the same time. Here is my business card."

Sarah glanced at the card and noticed that it said: Hollingsworth & Son. "You have a son?" she asked quizzically.

"Oh, no," he laughed. "I'm the son. My father started this business many years ago. My dad's health has been declining and I've pretty much been running the business as of late. I probably need to have new cards made up or I'll have to get married and have a son real soon."

Sarah smiled, "I'm sorry I didn't mean to pry."

"No problem," he replied. "Say, how's your leg doing after that fall?"

"My leg? Oh, it's fine," she answered feeling her left leg.

"Good," responded Jim. "Sarah, I don't want to be rude either, but I do have another appointment to rush off to."

"That's fine, I'll call tomorrow," she replied getting up.

On her way out she said bye to Beth; and was soon back in her vehicle. Sarah reflected on how well it went and was happily pleased.

The rest of the day seemed to hum right along on a positive spin. Even her sister returning from school was having a good day. And for her mom, well, things were okay.

Next morning, Sarah, anxiously anticipated finding out who the owner of that particular piece of land was. She had her notebook and pen ready when making the phone call. But Sarah was astonished when instead of giving her the information, he wanted to meet her, face to face. Jim wanted her to go to the

County Park and pick out a picnic table, any table, and he would meet her there.

Sarah felt uneasy about this strange meeting. She really didn't know this Jim Hollingsworth. He seemed to be nice enough. It was out in the public. So everything should be fine.

Arriving at the Park she was nervous. There were a number of people walking along the flower-lined walkways and a couple of families sitting at the picnic tables. Sarah picked a table that was away from the two groups. She felt another spell coming on and fought it off. It was a time she had to have her wits in place.

Jim pulled up in the parking lot. After a moment he made his way down the main walkway holding a rolled map and a file folder.

"Sarah, thank you for meeting me," spoke up Jim spotting her at one of the first tables.

"Mr. Hollingsworth, you have me in quite a quandary on what's going on," she replied.

"Just call me Jim. There's nothing to be worried about. The news that I have is one that I don't want other people to speculate on."

"What news?"

"That the property you were inquiring about—doesn't exist."

"What? It does exist! I've been there; you've been there," refuted Sarah.

"I know, but let me explain," he smiled.

"The property exists in reality, but does not exist on paper. Are you familiar with survey law or practices?" asked Jim.

"No, not at all," she answered.

"Let me see if I can explain this. First of all in the thirteen original colonies, the British system of metes and bounds was in use," he first started out.

"Metes and bounds?" queried Sarah.

"Yes, metes are straight line distances between points, measured in chains or poles. The orientation of these lines may be referenced by magnetic compass bearings or bearings based on true north," explained Jim.

"What is a chain or a pole?" she asked.

"A chain is sixty six feet and a pole is sixteen and a half feet," he informed.

"That's kind of odd, sixteen and a half feet," she questioned.

"That's a quarter chain," clarified Jim.

"Oh, okay."

"Now the bounds part of this is that some land descriptions followed natural or manmade features such as creeks, roads or stone fences for example. But what was common in all of this was they all had starting points, called the Point of Beginning. Even though two properties may be adjacent to one another they may have two different Points of Beginnings and in some rare occurrences the boundaries of the two parcels may overlap or even have a gap between them. This is called a hiatus. I believe, based on aerial photography and the legal descriptions of nearby properties including the one that I'm currently working on, that the blueberry patch falls in a gap, a hiatus, between two or more of these properties," he further explained.

"That's extraordinary," replied Sarah. "But why be secretive about this?" asked.

"If it could be proven that there is real property located in a hiatus and legal access can be gained to it, that property could be worth a small fortune," he answered.

"I see, but how is it that no one after all these years has caught on to this?" pondered Sarah.

"A basic reason could be that these were very large tracts of land originally, and no one was particularly concerned," theorized Jim. "Another reason could be that because of the river branches and the associated swamps it was an area probably of no practical concern. However, between you and me, there's something else that's odd about this property that I can't put my finger on as of yet. It will take further investigation."

Something that Jim wasn't aware of was that there was a hidden structure on the property and someone long ago did live there.

"But at this point," continued Jim, "this is all unproven. What should be done is an extensive survey to tie in all the survey monuments and control points in the whole area. That could be a lengthy job."

"That would be too much for me to get involved with," realized Sarah.

"There is an easy way we can test this theory without doing all of that," he reasoned. "No charge to you. This is on me. It's not so much the potential of making money on this deal, but I'm more curious what's really going on out there."

"Yeah, me too," she agreed.

"Hmm, Billy and I will be out on the property about nine in the morning. We are one person down on the crew right now. If you're available and willing to help we could make this happen," he proposed.

"Yes, probably, but can I have my sister tag along?" inquired Sarah.

"Oh, of course. More the merrier," smiled Jim.

That made her comfortable with the situation. It was best she didn't say anything about this to her mother. There would be too many questions.

"You'll have to show me what to do. I really don't know anything about surveying," she informed him.

"It isn't too difficult, just come appropriately dressed," he replied. "But concerning this matter, let's keep this between ourselves until we can get a better handle on what's out there."

"That's fine," readily said Sarah. "I always love a mystery."

After departing she thought about the deepening of this mystery surrounding the place where the wild blueberries were growing.

Her next problem was to convince Sadie to come on out to be with her.

What should I wear though? I have some overalls that were used for painting, which should work. They have lots of pockets. Would that be appropriate? Maybe, she pondered. Anyway, she was mentally racing ahead, but in the meantime there were more mundane things that had to be taken care of.

Next day Sarah was up early. She felt somehow different about things, but could not explain it. Sadie was slow to roll out of bed that morning and took a bit of coaxing to get her moving.

While driving over Sadie questioned Sarah about the overalls she was wearing. Sarah admitted she didn't know how to dress for the day's activity. Parking along the dirt road they walked the length of the meadow to finally spot Jim and Billy assembling gear next to a standing yellow tripod.

"Good morning," called out Sarah as they neared.

"Ladies, good to see you," replied Jim.

"No rescues today, right?" teased Billy.

"Actually, we're here to rescue you," countered Sarah.

"Oh, okay," he replied smiling.

"What's that you're wearing?" asked Jim trying to hold back a chuckle.

"Overalls!" she responded holding her hands on her hips. "I used them on my last paint job at home; and there is nothing wrong with them."

"No, I guess not," he laughed.

To get things started, Jim had everyone walk up to the adjacent property where they were to begin. Sarah noticed that a survey instrument was already positioned over a flagged iron pipe. Apparently this was along the easterly boundary of their current survey.

Jim explained they were going to run an open-ended traverse to the property monuments east of their location beyond the berry patch. While he set up the notes for the survey, Billy explained to the new-comers how to use a plumb bob, a prism pole, and the basic functions of a total station theodolite.

"This is quite interesting," realized Sarah who was caught up in a whole new world of discovery.

Jim double checked to see if the theodolite was level and over the point. She wanted to see how he turned angles with the total station, but he sent her and Billy up the line to set a back sight. Sarah learned how to set a paper target on an existing survey point.

After focusing on the back sight, Jim flopped the scope over and unlocked the upper motion of the theodolite in the general direction he wanted to go.

"These are called deflection angles," he explained. "Basically, it's a one hundred and eighty degree turn from the back sight, and then either it's an angle right or left. Next, Billy will show you how to drive a hub and set a new point."

About three hundred feet away Billy took a two by two piece of wood with a point on one end and proceeded to pound it into the ground until it was almost flush.

"Sarah and Sadie, just take a piece of flagging and fold it over like so," he demonstrated. "Carefully, take one of these long tacks, push it through the flagging and nail it into the center of the hub."

"Ha, just like a little flower," noticed Sadie.

Billy laughed. "The feminine perspective."

"It's a good thing," she replied.

"Sarah, take this prism pole and place it right on the tack. Use the fish-eye level to plumb up the pole and face the prism toward the total station. Balance it between your fingertips," instructed Billy.

"Explain to me what this is doing," requested Sarah.

"At this very moment Jim should be sighting on the center of the prism glass which will give him a horizontal angle. And at the same time the instrument is electronically measuring the distance to this point."

"That's amazing," commented Sarah.

"That's not all. If we preset the height of the prism, we can now calculate the elevation on our new hub," added Billy.

"It's all in the math," she realized.

"That it is," he agreed. "So Sarah, are you ready to go surveying?"

"Yes, let's get started," she spoke up excitedly.

4

NO MAN'S LAND

Sarah was a little slow in catching on at first, and found herself fumble-fingered in accomplishing most of the nominal tasks. As the morning wore on she was able to make some improvement. Sadie was right with her, learning and helping until she began to get tired.

Gradually, the traverse extended through the trees, down and around the blueberry patch and another quarter mile to the east tying into two existing property markers. The land beyond the blueberries was in a noticeable depression that seemed to meander like an ancient drainage off toward the Great Pee Dee River which was only a short distance off to the southeast. There was a gradual transition from the large sprawling oak trees to Bald Cypress along the edge of the swamp. Long beards of Spanish moss hanging from the trees waved like banners in the afternoon breeze.

"Thank you for coming out and giving us a hand," praised Jim as they walked back toward the berry patch.

"I didn't know what to expect, but I think I actually like this kind of work," remarked Sarah.

"After a little practice you were getting fairly steady holding a plumb bob," he commented. It further crossed his mind that she didn't complain about the work or the fact that she was getting her hands dirty.

Sarah looked back to see if anyone was within listening range. "How soon will you know what the results will be?" she asked.

Jim also turned around to see if anyone was close by while carrying the tripod and theodolite on his shoulder. "It might be two or three days. I have a couple of other jobs to close out," he replied.

"If I can help, let me know," she offered.

"I appreciate that, but I'll have to see," commented Jim.

Somehow she felt a little disappointed that he didn't jump at the chance to take her up on that offer. Usually, it was she who was the one putting other people off. However, she believed he wasn't doing it intentionally.

Sarah and Sadie went home dirty and tired. They had some explaining to do when their mother questioned them about what they were up to. Sarah showed her Jim's business card and explained it was all legitimate. She was concerned that Sarah was getting herself into another bad situation. But her daughter assured her that was not the case.

While the jury was still out on the disposition of the mystery property, Sarah considered what the approach might be to gain access into the stone cabin. There were heavy vines growing across the heavily barricaded doorway. What to do? She was not that handy with power tools. Sarah thought she could try using a hand pruning saw and see if that would cut through the vines. Sarah was determined to keep this part of the mystery to herself as long as possible.

Two days later she decided to venture out after classes to test to see if she could cut the vines by hand. Feeling that intimidation again, Sarah very carefully crept around the hole to arrive at the door of the stone structure. The vines were much larger than she remembered. But she was there to try, and try she must. After sawing for a minute or so, Sarah stopped due to muscle fatigue in her arm. It was actually painful. She wasn't used to this. Not wanting to give up, Sarah continued off and on for another few minutes.

"Whew! This is hard work," she spoke out.

While she rested, her attention was drawn to a large weathered beam half-hidden in the vines that was barricaded across the door. It looked to be about eight inches square. Then Sarah noticed there was a heavy chain, like one you would see on a ship wrapped around the beam. At that point she realized that removing the vines and the shrubbery was not going to allow her access into this structure. There was an even greater challenge facing her now.

Whoever had this place did not want anyone in there, and apparently no one had entered it in a very very long time. A number of generations no doubt may have come and gone. This mystery was continuing to grow even more on her.

Back to square one. Sarah thought she better wait and see what Jim's conclusion on the status of the property was going to be. Perhaps then, a better solution would become clear. Sarah still held on to the hope she could keep the cabin a secret and would be able to solve this mystery on her own. But that was yet to be seen.

Two days later, Sarah was getting kind of antsy. She had not heard from Jim yet. Then it hit her that she hadn't provided anyway for him to contact her.

Sarah waited to call the next morning which happened to be on Friday. Jim answered the phone himself, stating he was the only one in the office for a short time.

"Oh good, you can fill me in on what's going on," she requested.

"Yes, I'm glad you called," he replied. "What has come to light is quite extraordinary. It truly is—no man's land. There is a definite hiatus in and around the blueberry patch, and guess what else?" he asked.

"I don't have a clue," responded Sarah.

"The shape of this is quite unusual," disclosed Jim. "Normally, when this occurs it is usually just a strip of land, a gap between two adjacent properties, but in this case, it is shaped like a fat diamond lying on its side at the common point of four properties. Technically, it is called an equilateral quadrilateral."

"Wow, a diamond in the rough so to speak," she thought out loud. "Where do you think the center of this diamond is?"

"About two hundred feet south of our traverse line, back behind the blueberries in the trees where you fell in the hole," answered Jim.

"Really! That's interesting," she considered. Sarah immediately thought about the stone structure.

"There could be as much as ten acres involved in this, if my calculations bear up. But there is something very curious about all of this," he stated.

"What do you mean?" asked Sarah.

"Well, first of all, the dimensions on all of its sides are nearly equal, being about eight hundred feet more or less," stated Jim. "But, what's really interesting is that this hiatus is at the center of where all four properties meet. The four property lines from the north, the south, the east, and the west all connect to the angle points of the diamond, but remember it is lying down, not vertical. What happens for example, if you follow the boundary line that is coming in from the north, it is offset from the one coming in from the south about the distance of ten chains. They come in like spokes to a bicycle hub, but offset."

"My goodness!" she declared. "You're going to have to show me on paper. I'm having a hard time envisioning this."

"I'm sorry, it is a difficult thing to explain over the phone," he apologized.

"That's okay, I'm very interested in what you're saying though," replied Sarah.

"I guess the point that I'm coming to is that there is a difference between what's on the ground and what is written in the legal descriptions," continued Jim.

"Okay, I do understand that," she replied.

"I don't want to confuse you any further, but the way the legal descriptions are written, it's like if you folded the diamond-shaped figure into itself and end up with three straight lines, one running east and the other west, but offset connected by a diagonal in the middle," further described Jim.

"Now you have really lost me," confessed Sarah.

"Well, what you end up with is just a line that jogs over, no hiatus being apparent," he explained.

"I think I understand where you are going with this. You are thinking that this was no accident," she reasoned.

"Yes, it appears that the surrounding legal descriptions were purposely crafted to exclude this property. But why I do not know," he replied.

"Just a minute, my mother is trying to talk with me," interrupted Sarah.

Jim could hear her talking to an indistinct voice in the background. Apparently, she was curious as to whom Sarah was talking to.

"Jim, my mom would like to meet you sometime, she is asking," relayed Sarah.

"That would be fine," he answered mildly. "Since you and your sister were out the other day helping us and maybe again, that would only be appropriate."

"You would want me to come out and help again?" she asked a little surprised.

"There is a possibility. Experienced help is hard to come by, and you might be able to fill in for a while," answered Jim. "But please keep the preliminary results of the survey confidential for a time."

"Oh, yes, of course," she agreed. And at the same time she recalled that she also had to keep something confidential to herself as well.

This was quite unexpected having Jim Hollingsworth coming over to meet her mother. How did this come about? It was those wild blueberries that started all this she first thought. No, it was my curiosity and my falling into that stupid hole.

Which has set off a series of events that was taking her down an unknown road—to who knows where?

Two days later, following the directions he was given Jim finally found the Bentley residence. He drove up in his work truck; but was well dressed casually. As he walked up to the house he noticed colorful camellias and hydrangeas planted along the walkway. Knocking on the door Jim was quickly ushered in.

"Sadie, good to see you," first greeted Jim. Walking down a short hallway into the living room he greeted Sarah who was standing there with her arms folded.

"And you must be Mrs. Bentley," he presumed. "I am James Hollingsworth."

"Glad to meet you, Mr. Hollingsworth, please take a seat," she replied. "My first name is Bernice. You're a younger man than I had imagined."

Sarah seemed to be a little intimidated by this meeting. She continued to stand there, expressionless with her arms still folded.

"Where to begin?" started out Jim. "Sarah and I bumped into one another a couple of times and she showed some interest in land surveying. It so happens that I have a vacancy in the crew and I asked her if she wanted to come out and help, and see how it's done. And Sarah," gestured Jim holding his arm out toward her, "jumped at the chance if her sister could come out with her. And here we are."

"That's nice to hear," replied Mrs. Bentley. "Sarah hasn't been too communicative lately and I was just a little concerned."

Sarah was relieved and somewhat impressed with the way he explained things, leaving certain embarrassing things out of the picture.

"If there are no objections and Sarah is willing to continue helping us, we would love to have her for a while," further stated Jim.

"Are you are aware of Sarah's medical condition?" asked her mother.

"Yes, I'm aware of the spells that she gets from time to time. But that shouldn't be a problem," he answered.

"Well, Sarah," spoke up Mrs. Bentley looking at her for a reaction.

"Ah, yeah, I would like to get more on the job training. I'm finding it to be quite interesting," she answered.

"Or is it you're attracted to the boss of the company," teased Sadie.

"Sadie!" protested Sarah giving her a look.

"My sister was a tease also," commented Jim dismissing the notion. "Sarah, if you are really interested come prepared to work on Monday. You will receive pay, but it won't be much to start out with."

"That's fine," she happily replied.

"We can even work your schedule around any classes you might still have," added Jim.

The conversation continued as he largely talked about his family, the business, and community events.

After Jim left, Sarah's mom commented that he seemed to be a nice young man and seemed to be looking after her interests. Sarah thought about that for a moment, but relegated it to the fact that they were partnering up on the mystery property.

So, how was she going to proceed with gaining access to the stone cabin without divulging its existence to anyone else?

5

THE OLD LETTER

It was that phrase "no man's land" that Jim used that struck a chord in Sarah's memory. What was it that was of a similar nature? Then it came to her that something in the old letter that had been handed down in her family for a number of generations spoke of something very similar. The letter was interesting, but at the same time baffling. It gave cryptic details as to the location of a sunken ship or ships that were scuttled along the South Carolina coast. Some or all of these vessels apparently carried great wealth. Their location was a well-kept secret and its purpose was to buy British loyalty and perhaps even raise an army to combat the unrest among the colonists. Sarah knew from history and from the letter that this never happened.

Sarah had stashed the family correspondence among her things, since she took an interest in history and no one else in the family believed it to be solvable. She used it as a bookmark when doing research for classes on a number of occasions. Looking for the letter in her bedroom she found it in amongst a stack of history books in the volume "Colonial Empire – Foundation of a Nation."

It was still in its original envelop with a broken wax seal attached. Sitting in her desk chair she turned to catch the light from the window. Sarah opened it up and unfolded it, reading it through as if it was her first time.

August 18, 1783
William A. Bentley
King George, Virginia

To members of the Bentley Family may this letter find you well.

The subject contained herein is one of a highly confidential matter and much speculation is rife. Under the strictest secrecy, King George 111 dispatched four ships to the New World on about April of 1770 carrying cargos of immense wealth. The purpose of which was to prepare the way for a British invasion. However these ships were heavily damaged in a storm along the Southern Carolina coast. Most hands survived and were able to guide the ships into sandy hollows where they were buried in place. Key members who had overseen the final placement of this treasure are nearly gone. The committee as we call ourselves has been under suspicion. Even though we have mingled in among the colonists and have become part of the community, we have a deadly enemy. Because of fear that this precious cargo would fall into the wrong hands including insurrectionists claiming to be representing the British Crown, no action was ever taken. This sealed letter is to be delivered upon my passing so that this knowledge shall not perish with me.

The flagship's location is as follows: Where no land exists. Where north and south, east and west do not meet. Follow the path of the lion. Trust no one. When the danger has passed, use both keys, which will bring an agreed conclusion to this matter.

Signed,
William A. Bentley

No wonder no one has ever figured this out she thought to herself. If taken literally, it's not on land at all. But contrary to that, the letter did say that the ships were buried in place. However, the treasure was relocated to its "final placement."

A tingle went up her spine as she realized that where, "north and south, east and west," do not meet, and where "no land" exists must be at the blueberry patch. The clue was cryptic.

There was one final clue that could prove or disprove this theory—"the path of the lion." There were some odd looking marks on the stepping stones. Could this be true?

Imagine that! A whole ship could be buried under there somewhere. Wow!

The next day, Sarah couldn't wait for the sun to rise. There were so many exciting things happening, seemingly all at once. She was to start work that day; and there was even the potential of solving the mystery.

Sarah felt energized and was ready to take on the world. Beth even noticed her positive attitude when she came into the office. Jim was glad to see her, but he seemed to be preoccupied with business matters and was not very happy. Beth first had her fill out employment and emergency contact forms.

She was introduced to Carson Nash, the draftsman and also to Margaret Huff who worked in the front office with Beth. Carson was in his thirties, had a thin build and wore glasses. Margaret was more in her forties with greying hair and was very polite.

Afterwards, Jim gave her a tan surveyor's vest to use on the job. While this was going on Billy Montana was loading up the survey truck with equipment and stakes getting ready for the day's work.

Sarah noticed on one of the drafting tables a survey map that was partially drawn up. It was black ink applied to a plastic-like material that she learned was called Mylar. Bearings and distances were shown around the boundary of the parcel along with numerous printed certificates.

"Sarah, time to go," called out Jim from the back door.

"Okay," she replied turning to go out.

"Hop in the back," motioned Jim.

The backdoor of the two-seater truck was left ajar for her. Sarah scooted in next to a large square case that contained a survey instrument. Buckling up they were on their way. Their destination was just out of town in the rolling hills.

"Sarah, you'll be learning how to do differential leveling today," spoke up Jim as they drove along.

"Not sure what that entails, but I'm willing to learn," she replied looking out the side window.

"One thing about it you have to be very level-headed," joked Billy.

Sarah subconsciously reached up and felt the top of her head. Billy laughed.

"Are you poking fun at me?" she asked.

"Poking, no, maybe just a little ribbing that's all," he replied.

"Just don't start up with the dumb blonde jokes," insisted Sarah.

"Billy is quick with the jokes," explained Jim. "But we can put Billy on notice that we'll catch him on the next one."

"Sarah kind of laughed, "Yeah, I guess so." She reminded herself what working with men was like.

Arriving at the jobsite, Billy got out and opened up a wire gate so they could drive back in. Climbing a small knoll, Jim stopped on the top, which gave a commanding view of the entire property.

Jim asked her to find the small tripod in the back of the truck and set it up. He also instructed Billy to get both rods out. Sarah unbuckled the tripod and unlocked the legs allowing them to extend. After relocking them she placed the tripod next to the truck. Jim removed the level from the equipment case in the backseat and attached it to the tripod.

"Sarah, just a few minutes of instruction before we start. First this is a Zeiss level," he indicated placing his hand on the instrument. "To level it up use these three thumbscrews to bring the bubble into the fisheye," pointed Jim. "Next, what you will be more concerned with will be these two rods, the Philadelphia rod and the Linker rod."

To Sarah they looked like giant thermometers. The Philadelphia rod was made of wood with a metal face marked off in hundredths of a foot. The Linker rod was mostly made of aluminum also with a metal face.

"The Philly rod measures the elevation distance from the ground up to the center of the scope on the level. But now the Linker rod is a different kind of animal," explained Jim.

"It doesn't bite does it," teased Sarah.

"No, not unless you don't pay attention on how to handle it," he responded.

"Oh-h, sorry, I'm listening," she responded.

"It has a continuous ten foot tape that loops all the way around," continued Jim. "You may wonder, who created this confusing mess. But it does have its advantage at times. Especially, when there is the need to take repetitive shots on flatter terrain. It is also called a direct reading rod, because we can set the tape to a known elevation. Just place your thumb along the side opposite the number the instrument man is reading on the rod."

"Or instrument woman," she interjected.

"Yes, that could be," he agreed. "Next unlock the tape like so and slide the movable face around until you get the new elevation dialed in. The instrument man will check it one more time before waving you on. And that's it," finalized Jim.

"Okay, it'll take a couple of times, but I think I can master that," believed Sarah.

"But first we're going to run a benchmark circuit around the property using the Philly rod," he further informed. "Billy will show you how to set up a turning point, and how to wave the rod. After that we'll set a fifty foot grid and shoot the elevations later in the day."

And so it was Sarah and Billy set off to begin a level circuit that worked its way just inside the property boundary. Near the back end of the property a flock of wild turkeys meandered out of the tree line and slowly moved off on their approach. After an hour and a half they closed the circuit and returned back to where they had begun.

Sitting in the truck Jim began reducing the notes while Sarah rested. "I'll show you how to set up level notes and how to reduce them a little later on," he mentioned.

"I do have pretty good printing," replied Sarah without trying to sound boastful.

"Probably better than mine," smiled Jim.

Sarah was dying to tell someone about the old letter and the stone cabin, but she still wanted to check out the stepping stone clue first. She also came to the realization that without help she wasn't going to succeed in getting into the structure.

The rest of the day was spent running elevations on the fifty foot grid throughout the property. Billy and Sarah both ran a rod which made the process go so much quicker.

Sarah went home dirty and tired that evening. The next day was the same. She realized she had never worked so hard in her life.

After classes on the following day, Sarah made her way out to the blueberry patch to examine the stepping stones. Carrying a trowel and a whisk broom she ventured down through the meadow to the blueberries and quickly located the first stone. Scraping off the dirt revealed more of the stone. Using the whisk broom she was able to clean the fines out of the depressions. What Sarah now saw was what appeared to be large cat prints with claw marks.

"Lion paw prints, it has to be," Sarah told herself.

Proceeding to the second stone at the base of a large oak tree she stopped short at the sight of a very large Carolina Wolf spider sitting on a broken section of the stone.

"You are not going to scare me you little monster," declared Sarah picking up a stick and dispatching it into the brush.

The impressions on the broken sections also matched what was on the first stone. This had to be the site of the buried flagship, Sarah thought to herself. She looked around the terrain wondering where it was buried. But the answer was right in front of her, "the path of the lion." The path led to the stone cabin and that she was sure of.

"Time to go to the next chapter on this," Sarah told herself.

Before leaving she decided to gather a sample of the blueberry plants to determine what particular variety these were.

Sarah knew she had to move on this. And so it was the next day she arrived at the office with the old letter in hand. Sarah believed she could trust Jim, but there were other men she also thought she could trust.

"Good morning, Sarah," greeted Jim as she came in.

"I'm hoping it really will be a good morning," she smiled.

"And what do you mean by that?" he inquired.

"Read this letter," requested Sarah.

"Okay-y," he acknowledged.

Sarah watched his facial expression as he read. She could tell it caught his attention. He repositioned his posture as he read on. After reading it he focused on her.

"This has been in your family for a very long time I take it," he stated.

"Yes, and no one has ever figured out where this is, until now," she answered.

"You don't mean your mystery property where I rescued you?" asked Jim.

Sarah looked around to make sure no one else was in listening range. "Yes, as you found out, it is uniquely 'no man's land,' and the final clue about the 'path of the lion,' is imprinted on the stepping stones that leads back into the trees," she confirmed.

"What about the keys that are mentioned in the letter?" he inquired.

"I believe there was a key that accompanied this letter, but I have no idea where it's at now," Sarah recalled. "And as for a second key, I really have no idea."

"Oh, additionally," she continued, "there is another thing that I have not told you about. Further back hidden in that tangle of trees is a stone structure that is totally overgrown and barricaded from the outside."

"So, that's why you were nosing around back in there in the first place," realized Jim.

"This is true, but it wasn't until you discovered this hiatus that things began to fall together," replied Sarah. "It's going to take some work to get into the stone cabin. I need your help."

"You are my client in this matter," he confessed.

"Yes, and you are my boss. But I need something more out of this relationship than that," she argued.

"Oh really? What are you proposing?" asked Jim.

"A partnership I guess. Fifty-fifty on everything," answered Sarah.

"Partners then," he replied holding out his hand after a long pause.

Sarah shook his hand and smiled.

6

FUZZY HISTORY

"Okay, Miss Bentley, we also have other work to do today as you know," stated Jim handing back the letter.

"Project 'Stone Cabin,' or whatever we want to call it, is confidential just between us, right?" she asked. "That is for now."

"Definitely, we'll have to move on this cautiously. There are legal and historical issues that we will have to navigate around," he answered.

"What is it we're navigating?" asked Billy who just walked in.

"Our way out to the truck to start with," answered Jim being evasive.

Sarah smiled knowing everything had gone well and there was yet to be more discoveries to be made. She liked this feeling. It was something she could get used to. This positive motivation stuck with her the rest of the day.

The day's work took them to a remote piece of property that had been previously surveyed, but lacked the final monumentation and the filing of the Record of Survey at the County Recorder's Office.

Jim set up the total station on a control point on the interior of the property. Sarah gave him a backsight on a reference point along the perimeter. With a readout of the angles and distances he had Sarah move in a counterclockwise direction setting a stake wherever a permanent monument was to be set. Billy was following right behind pounding a section of ¾ inch iron pipe into the ground. After which he would insert a yellow plastic plug into the top of the pipe with Jim's land surveyor's number on it.

Sarah was quickly moving around the property setting various angle points and corners using a prism pole. She was more than half way around, and Jim again directed her on to the next location using hand signals. Looking through the scope he waved her left and even further left until suddenly she disappeared out of sight.

"Sarah!" he called out.

Looking several hundred feet across the clearing she was nowhere to be seen. Jim began running across the field fearing Sarah may have fallen into something again. Instead he heard her laughing.

"Sarah, you okay?" he called out.

"Yes, I'm fine," she responded.

Jim spotted her lying on the ground sitting up.

"I'm sorry," she chuckled. "It's just funny. I'm watching you. I'm watching the terrain. Back and forth, and suddenly boom! I'm down on the ground."

Jim extended his hand and helped her up. "Everything still in working order?" he asked.

"I'm still in one piece," she answered dusting herself off. "Jim, my working with you somehow has been good for me. I want this to keep going."

"That's nice to hear, but you need to watch your step, young lady. I don't want to lose my partner," he smiled walking back to the instrument.

A tingle went up her back as she imagined something more out of that comment. Yes, I want this to keep going too, she told herself.

Come Friday night an event in town happened that signaled the start of serious trouble for the community and potentially for Sarah and Jim as well. The next morning Sarah heard that the Track of the Lion Tavern had been broken into overnight. That made her curious. It's name was so similar to the 'path of the lion' clue. Was someone else trying to follow clues to the site of the treasure ships or was it just coincidence? She had never thought of this particular connection before. The Track of the Lion Tavern had been there forever it seemed. The old blue faded sign at the front of the building made the claim that it had been in business from the year 1780. The owner of the business was a friend of the family. Sarah thought she would stop by and see what happened and snoop around a bit.

Located near the marina, the old inn was situated along a row of businesses across the street from the harbor. Parking down the street, Sarah made her way along the sidewalk passing the shoe repair store and Mr. Brewer's bait shop. Approaching the tavern she made out the presence of yellow police tape that now had been pulled off to one side. A pile of broken furniture and debris was being deposited just outside of the entryway.

Sarah poked her head in the doorway to see someone sweeping up broken glass. Stepping inside the poorly lit room her eyes adjusted to see damage everywhere.

"Sarah Bentley!" rang out a voice from the darkness. It was the owner of the tavern, the elderly Mr. Rossi, a short gentleman of Italian descent.

"Hi," she greeted.

"Young lady, what are you doing here?" he asked.

"I heard the report and was curious as to what happened and who did this," answered Sarah.

"No one knows who did this or why," he answered in a perturbed voice. "The police came and looked around, but they couldn't figure anything out. The worst damage is down in the basement. It's almost like they were looking for something, but I have nothing to hide," declared Mr. Rossi.

"I'm sorry this happened," consoled Sarah.

"Mr. Rossi?" came a loud call from the doorway.

"Yes! over here," he yelled back.

Apparently, from what Sarah could gather the visitor was an insurance agent. Mr. Rossi excused himself to talk with him. This interruption served Sarah well. It gave her an opportunity to poke around for clues.

Walking through the main dining area she noted that many of the small tables and numerous chairs were all knocked down and shoved to the back of the room. In the kitchen, all the cabinet doors were left ajar and much of their contents pulled out. Back in the storage room, standalone shelving had been pulled out from the walls and much of its contents had fallen onto the floor. It was apparent that whoever did this was looking for something along the walls. Taking the stairway she made her way down into the basement to see even more devastation. Wine racks were tipped over making a terrible mess. Broken glass and pools of wine made it a challenge to walk around, but again it was evident that the attempt had been made to examine all the walls in the room.

The walls themselves were principally made up of layered stone and a section of old brick toward the back. It was this brick section that drew her attention. A number of bricks had been busted out to reveal soil behind. There was a clear distinct shape of an arch in the brick wall about two and a half feet off the floor. It was within that outline that the vandals had broken out the bricks, probably hoping to find a tunnel or something. Sarah realized it must have been an old Dutch oven, which abandoned and sealed off quite sometime in the distant past.

It was Sarah's conclusion that if the crooks were looking for clues to the locations of the old shipwrecks they did not find them here. Bumping a brick on the floor she looked down and in the dim light spotting something white. Reaching down, Sarah picked up what looked like a crumpled business card, but there wasn't enough light to read the printing.

Putting it in her pocket she made her way back up to the main floor. Mr. Rossi and the insurance agent were still in conversation about his coverage on the vandalism. Sarah could tell he was getting quite perturbed at what he was learning. Discreetly she made her way back out not bothering them.

Once outside, Sarah pulled out the business card and turned it to the light to read what was printed on it. She made out the words: Southern Treasures. Sarah recognized that name. It was a local pawn shop that dealt in gold and coins. On the back was what looked to be a faint address scribbled in pencil. She wondered if this was a clue to the identity of the vandals or was perhaps nothing at all. She tucked the card back in her pocket and headed back to the car.

A couple of days later, Jim met with Sarah to discuss how they should proceed with their investigation on the mystery property. He strongly believed before they physically cut their way in and entered the stone building, they should first do a detailed title search on the property. This would identify any legal entanglements or claims of ownership that could potentially stop them dead in their tracks. Sarah agreed and realized she would have to be patient if they were going to do things the right way.

Jim took her by the Courthouse briefly one morning to show her how to look up property descriptions and their reconveyance in the Official Records which dated back to the year 1769. Before that all records were filed in Charles Town now called Charleston. History was one of Sarah's interests and she believed this could be quite an interesting journey into the past.

Coming back on her own the next day she began a title search starting with the four current properties in the area. She looked up repetitive Grantor-Grantee references that listed each time the property changed hands. These references were in alphabetical volumes weighing about twenty five pounds each.

There were also other people in the Recorder's Office looking up records, probably from the different title companies in town. One thing that was particularly annoying to her, and which was especially noticeable with the men, was the tendency for them to slam the books closed when they were done. It seemed that this was some form of intimidation on their part for her entering into their domain.

Nevertheless, Sarah pushed on to see, who, when, and what was involved in the sale of each property. To do so she had to look up how it was recorded in the equally heavy Official Record volumes. Initially, most of the pages were type-written, but as she proceeded further back in time they were all written in cursive handwriting. Some of which were very beautiful in compact sweeping letters. Even further back the penmanship changed to quill pens that often skipped and faded, which made readability a little more difficult.

Sarah looked up at the clock and realized it was almost time for the office to close. She felt good about what she was able to accomplish on this first visit.

She shared with Jim what progress she had made with the title research, and the antics of the others slamming the books closed. He laughed knowing exactly what she was talking about.

It would be another three days before Sarah could return and do more searching in the records.

Between her classes, working part time, and doing the research she found herself extremely busy, to the point that her mother and sister seldom saw her during the day. Sadie missed Sarah's companionship now that she was working. Perhaps on some level Sadie was a little jealous of her new preoccupation.

A few days before, Sarah had brought into her botany class a sample of the blueberry plants. After class, Professor Everhart helped her determine what variety they were. Looking through a journal of botanical illustrations, the determination was made that they were a European variety. The Professor commented that this should not be of any surprise since many of the colonists would have brought them over. For Sarah this was validation that there was something special about that site.

Two days of surveying that followed proved to be physically taxing on her. Sarah estimated she had covered several miles traipsing through the Indian grass and even had a run in with a Black Racer snake. It was non-venomous, but nevertheless it had scared her something fierce.

It felt good to finally get an afternoon off to do further research. The women who worked in the Recorder's Office took note of her presence again and probably assumed she was now a new regular.

Placing her notes on the table top she began where she had left off, in about the year 1910. Each reconveyance of the original four properties used the same land descriptions. These were what undoubtedly Jim used to compare against the reality of what was discovered during the land survey. As he said, the metes and bounds description of the four pieces of land seemed to run along common lines to common points. No hint of a hiatus was given.

But now, as Sarah dug a little deeper the four parcels finally became two. In the year 1813 there had been two large tracks of land that were being split north and south breaking the land into four. This was long before the Civil War she realized. Sarah noted a significant change in the description of the north-south line that ran up through the middle of the two rectangular parcels.

Going back further into the Plantation Era, Sarah's research took her past 1776 when the British first attacked Fort Moultrie at Charles Town and the Declaration of Independence was made in Philadelphia. Reinforcing the Americans positon, the French in 1778 formed an alliance with the rebel nation and declared war on Britain. From her history lessons she recalled that in 1780 the British had attacked and captured Charles Town. South Carolina happened to be the richest of the original colonies. But in the ensuing year American troops advanced toward the city and forced the British to abandon it in 1782. The next land change occurred in the year 1771. Apparently, this was when the original tract of land was split in two. What was it that Jim said about the north-south line? That it had a jog in the middle of it? Well here it was described as follows: "Thence running on a course due north forty chains more or less to a point beside a branch of the Great Pee Dee River; thence north 45 degrees east twelve chains crossing said branch of the Great Pee Dee River to a point beside the branch of said River; thence due north forty chains more or less to the south line of lands owned by Jedidiah Brimwell."

Sarah could see how there could be a purposeful confusion between those two points lying on either side of the branch of the river. When the land was split four ways, the north-south line coming from the west would connect to the northerly point and the line coming in from the east would connect to the southerly point. The jog itself was to make a crossing of the then existing branch of the river apparently at an oblique angle. If she understood it right, the twelve chains crossing the river would form the bottom right-handed side of the hiatal diamond.

Sarah gasped to herself as she had a flashback memory of standing there by the blueberry patch noticing a depression in the ground that seemed to wander off toward the Great Pee Dee River. "Yes! It is true. I've seen it," she told herself.

The date also made real sense. Because one year before, was when the fleet shipwrecked during the great hurricane. Sarah realized this was as far as she needed to go. But she had to make sure that there were no partial interests left tangling in the chain of ownerships somewhere. Sarah also made a note that a certain James Bakehart, was the owner of the original tract of land.

On the way home she thought about the jog in the north-south line crossing the long forgotten river branch and contemplated where that was in relation to where the stone cabin sat. It could very well straddle the north-south line or at least be very close to it.

Next morning, Sarah arrived a little late at her history class, and was surprised by the lively discussion that was in progress.

Someone had brought an article from the town newspaper. The headline read: "Search for Local Legend Gets New Life."

The article pointed out that after the last hurricane a number of relics had become uncovered, which spawned speculation about finding the buried loot from an old ship wreck that occurred before the Revolutionary War.

Wow! The information contained in the old letter was not just exclusive to her family. It was already out there. Apparently, it was also well known during the Civil War. The South was no doubt hurting for revenue as the war progressed. A search had been made, but nothing was ever found.

An unnamed source claims that a recent discovery in the British Archives showed that Georgetown was the approximate area where the stash was buried, but no exact location was given.

The question was posed in class: "Why did the British only have a general location if the loot was theirs to begin with?" Someone suggested there may have been some kind of subterfuge carried on by the survivors of the ship wreck. They were closer to the truth than they knew.

Sarah was now alerted to the fact once again that others were also in the hunt. Matter of fact, just as she had observed not that many days before, there was someone out at the blueberry patch looking around with a map and there was the break-in at the Track of the Lion Inn.

This simple little mystery about the stepping stones and the stone cabin had suddenly crossed a line. But in a sense she felt she had been handed the key to unlock the mystery. Speaking of which, where was that key that came with the old letter? Sarah set her mind on finding it, because soon they would try to enter the stone cabin.

Back home, Sarah asked her mother if she had any recollection of where the key was that came with the old letter. She recalled it had been hanging on a nail above the workbench in the basement some years before.

"Oh, good," she responded getting up to take a look.

46

"What do you want with that old key?" questioned her mother. "You still trying to figure that out?"

"Possibly," answered Sarah as she disappeared down the steps that led into the basement.

Making a beeline for the workbench she searched through the items hanging on the wall and above the bench, but it was not there. That was discouraging. Where could it have gone? There were numerous boxes shoved under the bench. Sarah spent a long time carefully searching each box to see if it had fallen into one of them, but again it wasn't there. About to give up, she turned around and glanced back toward the stairwell and there it was attached to a beam about four feet out from the stairs.

"Now who did that?" wondered Sarah.

Reaching up she unhooked it from a couple of protruding screws. It was a large fancy skeleton key with a B formed in the handle part. "Yes!" she thought to herself, "one down, and one to go."

She had much to share with Jim; but she was especially anxious to find out what was in the stone cabin. She needed to be careful not to say the wrong thing that would dissuade him from continuing on with this.

7

THE STONE CABIN

Jim was satisfied with the results of the legal research and saw no reason why they couldn't make a cursory inspection of what was on the untitled property, besides the fact that surveyors by law were allowed to enter private property for surveying purposes. Though he thought he might be stretching it a bit, Jim felt that there should not be any problem. So they decided on a Saturday when there was no work or classes to go exploring. Sarah wondered if they could invite Sadie out, because she felt that her sister was feeling neglected. Jim agreed, and thought she could be trusted, since Sadie kept quiet about Sarah's accident out at the property.

Sarah decided to prepare a picnic lunch since Jim was going to provide the power equipment and the manpower to get the job done. To Jim it sounded like she was planning a family outing or something. Sarah commented if that was true, their daughter would be almost as old as she was. Jim laughed, agreeing that would be a biological impossibility. For her, just the discussion of having a family gave her a warm glow on the inside. She wondered if this was normal for hormones to produce such affects?

Jim additionally recommended that while they were working back in the trees near the cabin, they should go ahead and fence off the hole that Sarah had fallen into. He recalled having four

'T-bar' posts that he had at home and a length of rope that would form an enclosure.

Anticipation for the day was building, so much so that it was hard to focus on anything else. However, passed the hype, she had to consider that once the door was opened that there may be nothing of significance to be found.

The morning finally came and it turned out to be a bright sunny day, ideal for working under the shadowy tree canopy. Their plan was to meet at nine in the morning. By the time Sarah and Sadie arrived, Jim had already made one wheelbarrow run of equipment and supplies over to the blueberry patch.

"How's my sunshine girls doing today?" he called out seeing they had arrived.

"Slow to rise," yawned Sadie.

"I'm doing well," answered Sarah.

At times she didn't know how she should address him. There was a connection between them, more than an employer-employee relationship, and more than a business relationship.

Jim helped them carry the picnic gear down to a shady spot. While they were setting up he went back for the final load.

When he returned, Sarah showed him the key that she had found in her basement.

"Wow, that is one ornate key," he commented. "It even has a B on the gripping end. B is for Bentley, right?"

"Yes, I believe that is correct," she answered.

Sadie set up a lawn chair where she was going to occupy her time reading a book while Jim and Sarah were working.

It took a few minutes to do a final maintenance check on the chainsaw. Next was the task of packing in the equipment and the fence posts to a second staging area back in the trees.

Looking at the task at hand Jim thought first to clear the vines that would allow the four fence posts to be driven in.

"Sarah, because we're working in such tight quarters, I want you to stand behind that big limb back there while I do the cutting," he instructed. "Wear your googles while the chips are flying, and use these ear muffs also. "Once I shut off the chainsaw come back in and help me pull the limbs and the vines out of the way."

"Okay, boss," she replied.

Jim smiled, "Just call me Jim."

"Sometimes I have to remember which hat you're wearing so I know how to address you," she confessed. "I get confused, because you are my boss, and you are also my partner."

"Just, Jim, will do," he reiterated.

Firing up the saw he proceeded cutting away limbs and vines that would be in the way of setting the posts. After about four minutes Jim shut off the saw and removed his ear muffs and goggles.

"That oughta do it. Sarah, make sure you stand well back from the edge of the hole," he cautioned.

Putting on her gloves she ducked under and started pulling the cuttings away from the hole. Jim grabbed a steel fence post and positioned it. Using a two-handled rammer he hammered the post in a short depth with a loud metallic clang. Setting a second post he set that one as well.

Sadie worked her way back and poked her head through the branches inquiring what that dreadful noise was. Sarah explained that Jim was hammering in fence posts to rope off the infamous 'hole in the ground.'

"Oh, okay, good idea," commented Sadie who subsequently went back to her book reading.

After finishing that project it was time to focus on the main event. Again Sarah stood back while Jim opened up a short corridor that led up to the rock structure. Turning off the saw again, he could get a close up look at the large wooden door and a large oak beam that ran horizontally in front of the door. The ends of the beam were interestingly inset in a protrusion of the stone structure. The beam itself appeared to be covered in some kind of bituminous coating. In addition a heavy chain was wrapped in a spiral around the beam.

"Whoever wrapped this chain around the beam was trying to prevent someone from chopping into it," he commented to Sarah.

"How do we get past that?" she questioned coming over to get a closer look.

"The spiral of the chain would work against right-handers trying to chop into it. Somebody put some forethought into this," realized Jim.

Watching Jim run his hand between the chains to gauge their spacing, Sarah asked, "Can't the chainsaw cut between the chain wrappings?"

"That's what I was trying to assess," he replied. "The bar is thin, but if I am off just the tiniest bit it would ruin the teeth." Jim paused for a moment. "Sarah! I know what you're thinking."

"Really? And what would that be?" she asked.

"What we need here is a real chain-saw," stated Jim.

Sarah laughed. "You're funny." She took note of that quality and found it pleasing.

He didn't comment, but continued checking the chain spacing. "If I can make five or six cuts here in the center, the whole thing should just fall apart. Okay, safety equipment on, let's try this."

Firing up the saw again he surgically cut into the beam between the chain wrappings progressively working the tip of the bar further into the wood. Stopping he went to the next space, and went on to complete several cuts.

"There should be just a small wedge of wood holding it together," declared Jim after shutting off the saw again.

Grabbing a six foot limb of some weight he gave the beam a whack. There was a loud crack. Jim gave it another hit further to the left this time. Again there was a crack and this time a definite sag in the middle.

"One more should do it," he announced.

A loud pop was followed by the individual slices falling out between the chain wrappings allowing the beam to collapse in the middle. Once this occurred the heavy chain began to slide off of both sides and form a heap on the ground. It took a moment for the resulting cloud of rust to subside. The remaining ends of the beam hung down on the sides.

Sarah started clapping excitedly. "That was incredible."

"What are you guys doing back here?" questioned Sadie as she again reappeared. "What on earth is that?" she pointed.

"A stone building," answered Sarah. "It's been boarded up for a very long time."

"You didn't tell me anything about this," she protested.

"No, I wanted to keep this hush hush until we got to this point," her sister explained.

"How about a lunch break?" suggested Jim.

"Yes, that sounds good to me," replied Sarah.

Jim took a few minutes to clean himself up from the sweat and sawdust before venturing over to where the girls had the picnic lunch.

"What other secrets have you not been telling me?" asked Sadie while she unpacked the lunch.

"None, Sadie, there are no other secrets," declared her sister.

"You and Jim seem to be getting along quite nicely," observed Sadie, who seemed to be fishing for something more.

"Yes, everything is fine," she flatly answered.

"So, what are you girls talking about?" inquired Jim coming back over to join them.

"Oh, just chit chat," replied Sarah smiling. "Jim, you cut your arm," she noticed.

"Just a little bit, nothing serious," he replied. "Who knows, there may be more of our blood shed on this property in the future."

Sadie looked at Sarah and then at Jim, wondering what he meant by that.

Jim recalled that Sarah had said that her sister was feeling neglected and made it a point to converse with her inquiring about her likes and dislikes, and what interested her.

"Thank you for the fine lunch," complimented Jim.

"You certainly earned it," replied Sarah.

52

"Anyone ready to see what's in—the mysterious stone cabin?" he asked deepening his voice.

"Yes!" both sisters responded.

Carrying a crowbar and flashlights they made their way back into ground zero. Jim dragged the chain off to one side and dislodged the two remaining pieces of the beam to move those out of the way. A heavy metal latch probably made by a blacksmith held the rugged door in place by means of a tapered iron spike. Sarah noted that there was no key hole for her key to fit into on the exterior door. Jim hit the bottom of the spike with the crowbar and made it jump out of its keeper position. Sarah pulled on the door, but it was solidly stuck in place.

"Let's see if we can pry it open," suggested Jim.

Inserting the tip of the pry bar he gave it a shove. The door grunted and moved about an inch. The weathered wood at the door's edge frayed. Getting another grip he moved it again a couple more inches. Using the curved end of the bar the door was opened to about one foot. Finally, with some difficulty he was able to push it most of the way open, maximizing the amount of light that was able to shine in.

"Whew! What a dank smell coming out of there," declared Jim. "I hope there are no skeletons lurking in the darkness."

"Oh-h, don't say that," complained Sarah making a face.

"Sarah, you wanted to know what was in here. Are you ready?" he asked.

"Yes, I'm curious to find out," she answered.

"Flashlights ready? Hold your noses," warned Jim.

Venturing in first, Jim shined his light along the left wall to see a bare rock interior. The floor was made up of rough sawn boards that were common on old ships. A wet spot indicated that there was leakage through the timbered ceiling.

"What do you see?" begged Sarah.

"Not much, there's a table, a number of old chairs, a desk, and a cabinet. Come in and see for yourselves," he answered.

"All these furnishings are so old," commented Sarah, "very ornate."

"There are no windows, and so far no skeletons," observed Jim. "Wait! What's that standing in the corner?"

The girls screamed.

"Oh, must be a cloak or something," he chuckled.

"That's not funny!" they protested.

"I'm sorry, I couldn't help myself," apologized Jim.

Then Sarah broke down and laughed about it.

"Sarah! It's not funny!" reiterated her sister.

"I know, but he said it so innocently," she replied.

"Sarah, I'm beginning to worry about you," stated Sadie.

"The desk has an inkwell and old stationary all perfectly set and ready for use," noticed Jim.

"Umm," acknowledged Sarah as she too observed how the ceramic wear was placed in the cupboard. "It's almost like this room has been staged."

"Look at these old oil lamps," discovered Sadie. "The dust must be a quarter inch deep and full of dead spiders."

"Sadie, I believe you are technically correct," commented Jim. "They appear to have whale oil in them and not kerosene."

"These chairs don't match the table," realized Sarah. "They both have finials and were made during the same time period, but they are different."

"The table is extra-long," commented Sadie.

"I would almost guess that meetings were held in this room," figured Jim.

"Who were these people?" wondered Sarah as she focused her light on a carved sign on the back wall that read: Trust No One. Based on what she read in the old letter, that phrase made perfect sense. As she looked around again a sense of disappointment came over her. There was nothing here that made any connection to a buried treasure ship or ships.

Jim tried stomping on the floor boards going around the table listening for hollow sounds, but found none. Sarah carefully looked through the desk and the cabinet one more time to make sure they hadn't missed anything.

"Everyone seen enough?" asked Jim.

"Just a bunch of old antiques," commented Sadie."

"Yeah, I guess we're done here," Sarah disappointedly concluded.

8

FRIGHTENED

Sarah was sure she was on the right track, on the 'path of the lion.' Had something been removed from the old stone cabin that was a clue to the location of the buried ship's whereabouts? She didn't know what her next move would be. Had something gone undetected?

That week was the end of her semester classes which was a relief in some ways. She soon would be able to work full time on Jim's crew. It was definitely labor intensive, but the result had made her a stronger person. Matter of fact, for the first time she realized, she had not had a dizzy spell in quite some time. Wow! What else could it be, but this new employment of hers.

In many ways she looked up to Jim. Maybe there was something more here. There was that warm fuzzy feeling again. It turned her stomach thinking about it. Sarah told herself to stop and get a grip on herself.

To start out the week, Sarah learned about retracing old property lines that were established by magnetic bearings using a Jacob's Staff which was basically just a large compass mounted on a staff. She learned how to read the field notes and make the angular adjustments to compensate for magnetic declination that had gradually changed over the years. The person handling the instrument would first align to the adjusted bearing based on the compass needle and then sight through to put the chainman on line. If overhanging branches crossed the path, flagging was typically tied on to mark the alignment; otherwise an occasional stake would be set out in the open. She learned the duties of a head chainman on this kind of survey as they ran nearly a quarter of a mile.

Sarah was amazed how close they had come to an old stone monument. After cutting away the overgrown shrubbery, a three foot tall granite spire which leaned slightly was exposed.

"This has been here for a very long time," informed Jim.

"How long do you think?" asked Sarah.

"Nearly two hundred and fifty years," he replied.

"Wow, that's way back in the colonial days," she realized.

"This is where you can take your history lessons and interface out here with the real thing," commented Jim.

"Yeah, I'm interfacing with the real thing already, you guys," replied Sarah.

"Oh ho," laughed Billy. "The truth comes out."

Jim was surprised by that comment, but said nothing. Sarah sensed that he was taking it the wrong way.

"No, it's not you guys, it's just difficult for a woman to work her way up in a male dominated world," she explained.

"Sarah, I can understand that is perhaps what you have come away when studying history, but I know if you really apply yourself, there is no limit to what you can do," responded Jim.

"I like your optimism, but there seems to be a lot of cynicism in our culture," replied Sarah.

"All we can do is conquer, one person at a time those who have that cynical view," he laughed.

"Jim Hollingsworth! You're playing on my words!" she declared.

"Only if it works," returned Jim.

"Ah-hh! This is going nowhere," commented Sarah in frustration.

After work, Sarah had a sudden urge to do some investigating. She was not satisfied with coming up with nothing when they searched the cabin and wanted to take another look.

Without telling anyone she gathered a few things to take, including a light jacket; but only planned to be gone for an hour or so. Sarah noticed a few clouds to the south when driving over to park on the old road. The waning afternoon sun was becoming noticeable as she walked down the meadow into the shade of the trees near the cabin.

She packed a hammer, a pry bar, and a flashlight to assist in the investigation. The wind seemed to be picking up as Sarah made her way through the trees into the hollow that Jim had cleared out with the chainsaw.

Stepping in front of the cabin door she inserted the pry bar and gave the heavy door a jerk, but it only opened a couple of inches. Pushing on it again, it finally opened up all the way. Dull light filled into the black void. Suddenly a strong wind entered in among the trees catching her attention.

First order of work that she had in mind was to examine very carefully the inside walls in a clockwise direction around the room. The only thing that was found was an old smoking pipe wedged in a crevice. Using the flashlight again, Sarah searched the ceiling beams finding nothing unusual.

The winds outside were getting stronger making her a bit nervous. Sarah next focused on the old desk. Getting down she flashed the light underneath looking for anything hidden, but again there was nothing. Everything on the desk and in the desk were all perfectly set in place. Just as were the items in the cabinet and the cupboard; everything appeared to be staged.

A noticeable darkness now fell over the cabin. Stepping over to the doorway, it was apparent that the clouds she had seen before had moved in and had dimmed the sun. The winds continued to stir the trees. If her guess was right there was a thunderstorm brewing. That premise was verified when the sound of rolling thunder could be heard quite some distance away. She really did not want to be stuck out here during a storm, but on the other hand she really wasn't ready to give up either.

There were some items in the bottom of the cabinet that required more scrutiny. One of which was a large ceramic mortar and pistil. What was it used for? A number of large colored glass vessels also intrigued her. There were the remnants of something in the bottom of them. What possibly was it?

A bright flash of lightning and a loud crack of thunder brought her back to reality. The wind gusted causing the trees outside to hit against one another. Rain began to fall and it did so in a torrent. Sarah realized that she came totally unprepared for this. Lightning again struck down nearby and the thunder made her jump. Even if she wanted to leave, it was too dangerous to do so. It would pass Sarah told herself.

In the meantime, she went back to looking at a number of things in the cabinet and the cupboard. It wasn't long before the flashlight showed signs of giving out.

"Oh great!" she exclaimed.

Clicking the light off for a minute, the darkness seemed to close in around her. The lightning and thunder instead of passing over actually became even more violent. The flashing was intense, throwing moving shadows into the cabin. Like arms extended outward the shadows seemed to reach out to grab her. She felt a spell coming on. "No," she told herself. "I'm going to fight this." Sarah closed her eyes and tried to shut everything out.

But what was that noise? She popped her eyes open to look around. Turning the flashlight back on again she glanced around the room and out into the darkness. Was the sound coming from in there or was it echoing from a source outside? The way that the trees were moving about in the strong wind gave reason to believe that some of the large limbs were beating against one another. Illumination from the flashlight was now just a yellow glow. Standing to the right side of the table, Sarah turned around and tried to look at the back of the room, when a lightning bolt hit a tree nearby sending an instantaneous explosion of sound and light that caused her to jump and run across to the other side of the room. But in doing so something stopped her from behind, causing her to scream. Sarah panicked and pulled with all her might to break free. She heard something tear on her jacket and felt the resistance give way. In breaking free she plunged headlong into the wall and blacked out.

It was about six p.m. when Jim received a call from Sarah's mother wondering if he had seen her because she hadn't come home.

"She didn't make it home?" he questioned.

"No, and I'm quite worried, especially with this storm passing through," she answered.

Jim glanced out of the window at the storm that was moving through the area.

"Sarah, you wouldn't dare go out there by yourself would you?" he spoke out loud to himself. "Mrs. Bentley, I'm not one hundred percent sure, but I have an idea where she might be."

"Oh, good. Is it a place where I can go and check?" she asked.

"No, it's out at a place we call the 'blueberry patch.' Sadie knows where that is. I'll have to drive out there and hike in," explained Jim. "If her car is parked out on the road then I'll know she's out there. I have a couple strong lanterns that can light up half of the countryside."

"Be careful, it's still storming out there," she cautioned.

"I will, and I'll get right back with you either way, just in case we need to look further. But don't worry. I'll find her," he stressed.

"Okay, and thank you," she replied. "While you're looking out there I'll make a few more phone calls and check around."

Gathering up the lights and putting on his rain gear, Jim headed out to get in the survey truck. The lightning for the most part had moved off to the north, and the wind and rain also seemed to be abating.

Jim wondered to himself if she wasn't out snooping in the cabin, where else would she be? The knot in his stomach told him he was worried about Sarah and there were unaccounted feelings for her.

It wasn't quite dark yet as he drove out of his driveway. He could tell the sun was getting low behind the overcast. All the ditches along the roadways were still flowing full from the torrential downpour. Jim turned on his headlights and navigated the narrow two-lane roads out to where the old dirt road took off into the woods. The road was a little slick from the rain. A number of broken limbs had fallen onto the traveled way, but they were small enough to drive over or around.

After another quarter of a mile, Jim could make out the reflection of tail lights ahead confirming his suspicions. Coming up behind the vehicle he definitely could see it was her car. Jim tried the driver's side door and found it unlocked and the car empty. He peered out across the meadow in the dim light in the direction of the cabin. Hurrying, Jim got his gas lantern and his large battery powered lamp along with an extra overcoat gathered up.

There was enough light to walk down the meadow without bumping into anything. At the blueberry patch he lit up the gas lantern and proceeded to work his way into the cabin. A light shower rained down as he approached the door. It was wide open.

"Sarah!" he called out. "Are you in here?"

There was no answer. Stepping into the doorway Jim immediately spotted Sarah on the floor motionless facing away from him. Setting the lantern down next to her, he tried to revive her.

"Sarah! Are you hurt?" Jim gently pushed on her shoulder. "Sarah, can you hear me?" After a couple of attempts she finally awoke.

"Oh! My head," she responded reaching up to her forehead.

"You have quite a nasty bump," informed Jim.

"Jim! I'm so glad to see you," she exclaimed sitting up. "I need a hug."

61

"Yes, you can have a hug, " he answered complying with her request.

"I'm your princess aren't I?" she asked

Jim laughed, "Yes, you are my princess."

"Oh, I must have really smacked my head," realized Sarah. "I don't know where that comment came from."

Suddenly her facial expression changed to one of fright and her grip on his arm tightened.

"Somebody tried to grab me!" she declared looking around.

Jim grabbed up his other light and flashed it around the room, but could not see anything.

"Nobody here now," he reported.

"I was so frightened, the lightning and thunder, and the creepy shadows. It was almost like they were out to get me," recalled Sarah.

"You're safe now," he reassured. "The storm is gone and there is no one else here."

"Look, my jacket pocket got torn," noticed Sarah.

"It's getting cold, here put on my old overcoat. It'll warm you right up," encouraged Jim.

"Thank you. How did you know I was out here?" she asked.

"I had a good hunch," he replied. "Could this be what you thought grabbed you?" pointed Jim.

"The finial?" questioned Sarah.

"Something tore your pocket, and look how the finial has been pulled out," he noticed.

"That must be exactly what happened," she now realized. "Help me up."

After assisting her to stand and steady herself, Jim reached over and shoved the decorative knob back in and then back out. Jim stood there for a moment thinking about that. Stepping over to the other corner of the table he pulled the finial out at that location also. Going around to the backside of the table he tried the knobs at that end, but they were solid and did not move.

"Sarah, you may have accidently discovered something," he realized.

Coming around to the front side Jim tried lifting the table a bit. It made a loud cracking sound. Lifting it a little bit more, he noticed that it was made to lift up and pivot on the rear legs.

"A ship's table, perhaps," suggested Sarah.

Raising it up to about two feet off the floor, the front legs swung free and this time there was another loud crack in the floor just in front of them.

"Jim, you're on to something," realized Sarah. "Lift a little more."

As he did, a whole section of the floor was visibly separating itself from the surrounding floor. Jim lowered the table back into place.

"Sarah, whatever is hidden below the floor will have to wait for another day," he stated.

"Oh, must it?" she complained. "Oh, my head."

"That's the reason we have too," insisted Jim. "Your mom is worried sick about you and on top of it you may have a concussion."

"Yes, another day," she agreed.

9

HMS BLACKPOOL

"**C**an you walk?" asked Jim

"I believe so," replied Sarah.

Holding on to him they slowly made their way into the hollow. After closing the door, they carefully made it through the obstacle course of tree limbs and vines to finally emerge out by the berry patch.

"Sarah, it was not safe for you to come out here all alone," stated Jim after a long silence as they worked their way across the meadow by lantern light.

"My independent spirit would probably argue against that, but I think this time you are absolutely correct," she agreed. "Thank you for coming out and rescuing me again. Matter of fact, I can't think of anyone else who could come out and find me."

"If we're going to be partners in this deal, you're going to have to promise me not to come out here alone," he insisted.

Suddenly, two dark objects whizzed past them and disappeared into the woods.

"What was that?" asked Sarah.

"Just a couple of bats cruising for a meal," informed Jim.

"It's not going to be me," she declared.

After a thoughtful pause Sarah reflected on the nights events. "I'm sorry for jumping ahead. I just felt the urge to get this mystery solved," confessed Sarah.

Reaching where the vehicles were parked, Jim helped her get in the truck; and locked up her car. It wasn't long before they arrived at her home. Sadie and her mother rushed out to see if Sarah was alright.

"Sarah, what happened?" exclaimed her mother. "Oh, look at the bump on your forehead."

"I'll be fine. Apparently, I collided with a stone wall and I was not the victor," she explained.

"So, were you out at the blueberry patch?" questioned her sister.

"Yes, I was out there when the storm suddenly appeared," confirmed Sarah.

"I made her promise not to go out there alone anymore," added Jim.

"I hope you have better success in getting her to listen to reason than I have," stated Mrs. Bentley.

Mom! Everything is okay. Don't blow things out of proportion. Oh, my head," she replied heading for the bathroom.

"You'll have to keep an eye on Sarah for a while because of a possible concussion," advised Jim. "She asked me if she was my princess."

Sadie put her hand over her mouth and giggled. Before leaving Jim gave orders for her not to come to work for a couple of days.

By the time Sarah came back out Jim had already left. She was a little disappointed that she didn't get a chance to thank him again and return his coat which proved to be so warm and cozy.

Sarah's headache began to subside the following day and she was anxious again to get back to work and back out to the stone cabin as well. Sarah thought about how frightened she was out there. But when Jim arrived it dispelled all the gloom and doom that surrounded her. She felt safe to go back especially if he was with her.

Rising early, the next morning she judged it to be a typical humid day with a light coastal breeze. Sarah contemplated what she would first say to Jim once she arrived at the office. But when Sarah did arrive she was confronted with a bit of a surprise. There was a young woman in Jim's office laughing and talking about past experiences that they must have shared in the past. Beth believed she was an acquaintance of Jim's who just returned home from college. Beth smiled at her concern.

Why did this annoy her? Was this a sign of some kind of jealously on her part? Whatever it was it didn't settle well with her.

After the young woman left, Jim came out and was happy to see her there and doing much better. He didn't have much time to speak to her, but gave her and Billy an assignment for that morning.

Billy explained to her about engineering stationing and how to write up a survey stake. Apparently they were prepping for a construction job in town on one of the secondary streets.

He also mentioned that Jim had a meeting with an accountant that morning. According to Billy, Jim's father had been racking up the medical bills as of late, a lot of which his medical insurance would not cover. This was an aspect of Jim's life she knew nothing about. But it was enough to stop her from thinking temporarily about that woman in the office.

After lunch, Jim was back and ready to head out to the field. He was rushing around so much that there wasn't time to get an update on anything.

Once in the truck, after the initial conversations, Sarah had a chance to inquire about Jim's father and his well-being.

"He is not well," frankly stated Jim. "The doctors don't seem to know what's happening with him; and he's not getting any better."

"I'm sorry to hear that. I wish there was something I could do to help," she replied.

"That's pretty much the feeling of the whole family," he commented.

Arriving in Georgetown, just down the street from the Courthouse, the first order of work was to set up traffic cones around the survey monuments that they would be occupying in the center of the two intersections.

While Jim was setting up the theodolite on the first monument, and Billy was way down at the other intersection, Sarah thought it was a good time to approach him.

"I didn't get a chance to thank you again for rescuing me the other night," Sarah first started out. "And I apologize as well."

"You had me real worried," he confessed. "I don't like that feeling."

"You're having the same feelings for your father," she realized. "I'm sorry, I've added to your pain. Maybe I should just go away."

"Now stop," he declared turning away from the instrument. "Sarah, no, I'm overjoyed that you're okay and I don't want you to go away."

She could tell he was going through an emotional phase. He turned back to level the theodolite.

"You had a visitor this morning," demurely inquired Sarah.

"Maranda, yes. We dated for a short time and then she went off to college. I haven't seen her in about three years," he confirmed while looking through the scope.

She was hoping he would shed more light on what her intentions were, but Jim remained silent on that subject.

"Time to set a few hubs, Sarah, are you ready?" asked Jim.

"I is ready," she replied in a southern drawl.

"We'll be turning ninety degree offsets to opposite sides of the street at thirty seven feet. Use nails and shiners for the points that fall in the pavement, and Billy will use a gad and a sledge hammer to help you set the intermediate hubs," he instructed.

"Look, you almost had a 'beer leg' " pointed out Sarah.

"The tripod leg is almost on line isn't it," realized Jim. "But I prefer you don't drink much anyway."

"And why can't I do that?" she questioned.

"Because, you'll be telling everyone you are my princess," he laughed.

"Jim! You're not sharing that with others are you?" she wondered a little perturbed about that.

"No, we'll just keep that in the family so to speak," he answered. Jim thought it was wise to cover his tracks since he did reveal it to her mother and sister.

Sarah didn't know totally what he meant by that, but she felt it would suffice.

At the end of the day, Jim and Sarah made plans to meet out at the berry patch along with her sister and mother to chaperon the occasion, and make it into a weekend outing. Jim needed the next morning to help out with his dad, but afterward he could meet them out there.

While over at his parents' house, they were questioning him about the newest member on the crew, having learned it was a young woman. Jim gave them the story, a bit edited in places, but said he would have them meet her. His father didn't want to be left out of the loop that pertained to the business, and he thought his mother had other reasons to be curious.

Arriving at the usual parking spot, he was delighted to see Sarah's sister and mother come on out. They brought snacks, lawn chairs, and reading material.

"Lighting will be one of our most pressing needs," stated Sarah carrying over a bag that had a couple of flashlights and miscellaneous items.

"I brought along the gas lantern, and the large battery light once again," responded Jim. "I even have a small flash camera, if we ever find something worth photographing," he added.

Without much delay they grabbed up their gear and were off to the blueberry patch. After getting Sarah's mother and sister set up they ventured into the jungle of trees to reappear once again before the cabin door.

Jim opened up the door, and lit the gas lantern while Sarah went in and looked around. There was that sign again, "Trust No One," and the ornate table with its set of chairs.

"Ready to open the hatch?" asked Jim setting the lantern down.

"I'm more than ready," declared Sarah.

"You pull the first finial, and I'll do the second," he suggested.

Sarah, pulled the right front finial as she had accidently done on that dreadful night. Jim followed suit on the left side and began lifting up the table. The front legs were about three feet off the ground when a section of the floor measuring about thirty inches by forty-eight inches began opening up toward the back end of the table. As he raised it higher that section of the floor fell away and hinged downward revealing a dark hole. Careful not to fall into the hole, Jim pushed the table up past a vertical position where it stayed. The dank smell that permeated the cabin was even stronger coming out of the opening. Sarah coughed.

"That is so rank," she remarked.

"This has been sealed up for a very long time. No telling what we may find," he commented extending the lantern over the opening. "There are steps leading down," observed Jim. "Better let me go first."

Sarah did not object to that, but wanted to keep close behind. Jim pushed the hinged floor section up as he went down and was able to pin it in place above their heads. The only sound they could hear was the hiss of the gas lantern.

"Look, there is a second floor under here," noticed Sarah swinging her light around.

"That's interesting, their only about three feet apart," he observed.

A root was visible on the left side penetrating what appeared to be a wooden retaining wall that kept the soil from coming in. The steps creaked as they continued on down through an opening in the second floor. About eight feet below the second opening the steps led them down into a hallway. It ran in both directions and appeared to have numerous rooms adjoining it. Hanging from the ceiling and situated every so far were square glass lamps.

"What is this place?" initially wondered Sarah flashing her light in all directions.

"If I didn't know any better I would say we were inside an old sailing ship," stated Jim.

"Oh my, you're absolutely right," she realized. "What's wrong with me? That's exactly what we're looking for. The flagship is supposed to be buried here."

"Didn't the old letter say there was loot aboard this ship and the other ships also?" queried Jim.

"It's possible, but the letter did mention the treasure was being given a final resting place, so it might not be here anymore," recalled Sarah.

Their footsteps echoed as they proceeded to the first doorway on the left.

"Look in here, Sarah, all the oil lamps and lanterns stashed in here," discovered Jim.

"Wow! You have to see this. Over on this other side must have been the armory," she called out.

"Woo!" he exclaimed. "Look at that whole rack of vintage single-shot rifles and muskets. This is just like being at a museum. It's interesting though, they do appear to have a lot of wear on them," observed Jim.

"Further along, the sides opened up into cannon bays, with cannons still in place. Racks of cannon balls were in heavy timbered cradles.

"This is truly amazing," commented Sarah. "It's like we're on a movie set. But this is real."

They found what they thought to be the captain's cabin in a forward compartment. In the opposite direction there were rooms with British uniforms, and trunks that contained other clothing items, small arms and swords. Again the condition of the items were less than desirable. One brick-lined room was dedicated exclusively to the storage of black powder.

At a central location in the corridor an access point to a lower level was evident. The steps were steep and had no railing.

"I'll go down first and make sure the steps are still strong enough to handle our weight," he cautioned.

"I must admit it is good to have a man around at times," commented Sarah.

"That's a bit of a change from when I first met you," replied Jim.

"Yes, I have had a little change of attitude since we've met," she confirmed.

"The steps feel firm, so put your hand on the back of my shoulder and follow me down," he instructed.

Gradually the darkness vanished as they descended to the next level. Again a main hallway with some walls missing in certain locations ran most of the length of the ship. Appearing out of the gloom were dark silhouettes of more cannons frozen in time, poised for battle.

"This ship was definitely built for battle," commented Jim.

A bit further they entered into a large room at the back end of the ship.

"I believe this is called the 'great cabin' if my historical recollection is correct," stated Sarah.

"It's set up like a conference room or the like," observed Jim.

There was a large table with chairs, a small table, and cabinets on both the left and right sides. In the rear along the back of the cabin were shutters reinforced with cross members, indicating that there must have been windows behind them at one time. When at sea there must have been a grand view to the far horizon.

"Look at this on the wall," first noticed Sarah.

"What do you see?" asked Jim drawing closer. "Guardian of the Fleet. HMS Blackpool. The sun never sets on the British Empire," he read off moving the lantern along the wall.

"That must be the name of this ship, HMS Blackpool,"realized Sarah.

On top of a low cabinet that ran along the wall was a cloth bound volume located in front of the writing on the wall. Sarah flipped open the dust covered book. She coughed. Her flashlight spotlighted the handwritten words on the first page.

"Jim, read this," she demanded.

"What? For British Eyes Only," he read. "Wow, this might be what we're looking for. Besides, we both have English blood, right?"

She laughed. "Yeah, but I think we're well past worrying about that."

"I suggest we take this with us and not try to read it now," recommended Jim.

"I agree, we need to look around and see what else we can find," answered Sarah.

"Ah ha, look what is written above the cabinets on the opposite wall," he pointed.

"Trust no one," she read off. "Huh, it's the same as we seen up above. They must have been very paranoid. The old letter hinted at the very same thing."

Rummaging around the room they found an atlas, a number of sailing charts, and a couple of antiquated time pieces, besides various ceramic items, but nothing of significance.

On the same level was the ship's galley which included a brick-lined cooking enclosure, the ship's stores and the crew's sleeping quarters. Two more points of access were found that led down to the lowest level of the ship. Vertical ladders descended into the dark domain. Jim lowered his lantern into one of the holes to see what was down in the underbelly of the ship. He could make out, sailing rigging, rope, barrels of unknown content, and rock ballast. Also catching his attention was extreme damage to the hull of the ship on one side. Sand and soil had flowed in through the broken sections settling in the bottom.

"Well, I think we've seen about everything down here," concluded Jim. "A more thorough search may have to be made later if we can't find any other clues."

"No, we didn't find any precious metals, but there is a lot here that has historical significance," replied Sarah. "Perhaps the log book will be able to shed some light on all of this."

10

"FOR BRITISH EYES ONLY"

Jim and Sarah did not disclose that they had found a buried ship under the stone cabin, but did show Sadie and her mom an old book that they had found that no doubt had some historical value.

Sarah thought that despite the fact the land and the stone cabin did not legally exist, the reality was, it was going to be a real challenge to keep these things secret.

She took the volume home dying to find out what was written within. Jim said that was fine, as long as she kept the book in a safe place.

Come Monday morning Sarah came to work looking tired. Beth asked her if she had partied all night. Even Carson asked if she was okay.

"Sarah, you must have burned the midnight oil last night," also observed Jim.

"I did. I—" started out Sarah.

"Oh Jimmy, you are here," called out a high-pitched voice from across the room. Sarah instantly recognized that voice, it was Maranda. Her first thought was, "My goodness what is she doing here?" She felt annoyed by this distraction. Jim didn't need it and neither did she.

Jim noticed Sarah's dismay with Maranda's presence and smiled to himself. He spent a couple of minutes with her in his office talking. It seemed she was trying to set up a date with him. But from what Sarah gathered, from catching a word here and there, that he was real busy presently, but would consider it. That ruffled her feathers. Why didn't Jim just tell her to get lost?

Before leaving the office, Beth questioned Jim about the lights being on during the evening. Jim explained he had been doing some after-hours drafting.

Sarah was not aware he was working in the evenings. Jim motioned her over to the drafting table. He opened the drawer and partially pulled out a couple of Mylars and pointed to the lower right-hand corner. It read: Resurvey of Georgetown Plantation.

"Is this what I think it is?" she asked.

"It is," he whispered.

"I'm impressed," commented Sarah.

"Look here, the 'diamond,' " he pointed out.

"So, this is what our nonexistent land looks like," she said excitedly.

Jim put his finger up to his lips to remind her to be quiet about it. The shape was exactly like what he had described before, but now she could see how it existed in amongst the adjoining properties. It was a unique geometric anomaly.

"I have some exciting things to share with you out of the book we found, as well," quietly informed Sarah.

"Yes, but we need to get out to the field," replied Jim. "We can discuss it a bit later, if that's okay with my partner."

"Yes, boss," she agreed.

Jim laughed. "If someone was listening, they would definitely be perplexed by our conversation."

Later in the morning, they took a break and sat down on a short section of stone wall where she had a chance to share in private what she had come learn from the ship's log book.

"The ship's name is the HMS Blackpool as we read inside the ship, and it was the flagship of the fleet," confirmed Sarah.

"Blackpool, that's quite an intimidating name," commented Jim.

"The other three ships were called HMS Andover, HMS Bristol, and HMS York," she added. "I tried looking up British ship records on these four vessels, and guess what?"

"You couldn't find anything, right?" he guessed.

"Very little," answered Sarah. "There was a category of ships built by the British Crown for clandestine purposes, if you know what I mean. Documents were found that did list the proposed construction of the Blackpool, but no records exist that show that it was ever built."

"Interesting," considered Jim. "What else did you find?"

"The initial texts dealt with the fact that the ships and their contents were the property of the British Crown and were to be used only to advance the interests of Great Britain," she reiterated. "Any breach in that covenant would result in an unrelenting pursuit of capital punishment by the Crown and its representatives. Oh, I did notice also that the actual log of the ship's activities had been removed."

"Billy is coming, we'll finish this later," he spoke up putting his hand on hers.

A little tingle went up her arm. She realized that she was allowing herself to have feelings for him. In the past such feelings never worked out.

That afternoon, Jim moved the crew to another site. Their purpose was to tie-in various existing monuments with a number of property corners they had surveyed a couple of weeks before. Later Sarah learned that this was part of the Resurvey that Jim was putting together. He was accomplishing it little by little. She couldn't help but be impressed with his work ethic.

They agreed not to discuss their project on the telephone. The chances of there being eve-droppers were very great.

On the way back to the office, Jim asked if anyone had any objections to stopping by his father's house to drop something off. Billy thought it would be good to see his father again and see how he was doing. Sarah didn't have any objections. At the same time Jim remembered he promised to bring Sarah by so his parents could meet her. Perhaps it was a good time.

Pulling up in front of the Hollingsworth's modest home on a back street just out of Georgetown, they spotted Jim's father sitting out on the porch in a rocker.

"Sarah, my dad co-owns the survey company and would like to meet our newest crewmember," he coaxed.

"Oh, yes, gladly," she responded unbuckling herself from the seatbelt.

Trailing behind the other two, Sarah waited as they exchanged greetings.

"Sarah, I would like you to meet my father," introduced Jim.

"Glad to meet you, Mr. Hollingsworth," she spoke up. "I was concerned when Jim mentioned your health was not good."

"Oh, everyone is making more out of this than it needs to be," he replied. "It's good to meet you too."

Sarah mentally compared Jim and his Father. Though older and a little shorter with greying hair above the ears, he was nevertheless still a handsome man for his age.

Suddenly, the screen door swung open revealing a middle-aged woman. She figured it was Jim's mother.

"I thought I heard voices out here," she declared. "James, it's always good to see you, and Billy I hope everything has been going well for you," she greeted with a hug.

"Just like a summer duck," replied Billy.

"Mom, this is Sarah, and Sarah this is my mother, Joyce," introduced Jim.

"Glad to meet you," stated Jim's mother reaching for and squeezing her hand.

"I'm very pleased also," replied Sarah smiling.

"We heard that James had a pretty girl on the crew, but now I can see it's true," she related.

"Mrs. Hollingsworth, please, I'm just a humble flower of the Southern Coast," downplayed Sarah.

"James, where did you find her?" she asked.

"Sarah, should I tell them?" he asked.

Sarah put up her arms and gestured that it would okay.

"So, it wasn't through the traditional method," surmised Mr. Hollingsworth.

"No," laughed Jim.

"Jim, be nice," requested Sarah.

"Well, a couple of months ago, Billy and I heard a cry for help, and we came running through the trees where we found Sarah's sister who was quite upset. Apparently, Sarah had fallen into a collapsed cellar or a partially filled in well, and couldn't get out," explained Jim.

"Oh, were you hurt?" asked Mrs. Hollingsworth.

"Nothing serious, but that whole episode was quite embarrassing," answered Sarah.

"But anyway, Sarah demonstrated an interest in surveying and history, and she was also taking a few college courses at the time, so I thought to give her a try," he added.

"However it happened, it all seems good," commented Jim's father. "Jim has always been a good judge of character."

Sarah smiled, but made no further comment hoping to move the spotlight off of her.

There was a brief conversation about Mr. Hollingsworth's health, and then they were finally off.

Back at the office, after unloading the equipment, Sarah lingered a few minutes to talk.

"Thank you for not going into detail on having to rescue me a second time, or making some joke about finding me in a hole or something," stated Sarah.

Jim laughed, "That thought did cross my mind, but I reckoned it would not be in good taste."

"I appreciate that," she replied.

After a pause, Sarah, spoke up again, while Jim was going through his desk looking for something.

"Concerning the British volume, there is a section in there that gives clues to the location of the other buried ships," revealed Sarah.

"Really?" he exclaimed. "Is it something that we can follow up on?"

"Possibly," she answered. "It uses the phrase: 'A beacon, a rainbow of light shall show you the way.' "

"That could very well be the lighthouse over on North Island," reasoned Jim.

"Yes, and there are other clues that I think will bear that out," she agreed. "The first step that the book talks about is that we need to find something."

"And what would that be?" he asked.

"It's described as a mechanism, a Fresnel lens device, that when installed in the correct position would bend light to where the individual ships were buried. But there are only two locations designated," recalled Sarah.

"That would seem to suggest that two of the ships may be found at one of those locations," speculated Jim.

"The instructions to find this lens device are fairly simple. Count 70 steps up and find bricks with the letters, B, and H on them, or something of that nature," she tried remembering.

"You guys still here?" called out Beth from the front of the office. "I'm going home."

"Good night," replied Jim. "We'll be right behind you."

"Anyway, there is more, such as the manifests for all four ships," Sarah finalized.

"Anything of real value?" he asked.

She stepped closer to him and whispered, "When they set sail there were millions of British pounds of gold and silver currency distributed among the ships, but where it all ended up is yet to be discovered."

"Let's do this, you get those instructions typed up for those two locations, separately, and I will talk to someone about the Lighthouse and how we can gain access," planned out Jim.

"Yes, boss!" she responded.

"Oh, if that is okay with my partner?" he asked realizing he hadn't considered her input.

"That would be fine. And thank you for considering me," replied Sarah.

"There may be times when I may forget to take off my boss hat and put on my partner hat, so to speak," stated Jim as they made their way out. "And please get some rest tonight."

On the way home, Sarah had a bright idea. It would probably take three or four days to be accomplished. Seeing that one of the major department stores was still open she stopped and placed an order. They reassured her that she would be notified soon as the order came in. Sarah was obviously anxious to receive her special order.

Back in the car and heading home once again, she thought about the encounter with Jim's family. They seemed to be nice people. But it seemed she was being bombarded with everything that was Jim, his family, his work and his part in solving the mystery. He was in her thoughts when she got up in the morning and when she retired at night. Sarah asked herself am I losing my individuality. Am I losing my independence? And was this just happening much to fast?

11

THE SECRET OF THE OLD
LIGHTHOUSE

A number of days had passed since they discussed the possibility of the North Island Lighthouse being involved in the mystery. Sarah had the instructions neatly typed up and ready to use. Jim was still working on who to contact concerning the old historical structure. It had been closed up for some thirty years or more.

Originally, the island was donated in 1789 by a Paul Tropier, but it was in 1801 that the first lighthouse was built at that location. Its structure was made of native cypress standing some seventy-two feet tall until it came to its demise in 1806. It was in 1811 that a new more permanent masonry lighthouse was built. It was used as a refuge during the hurricane of 1822. And during the Civil War it was occupied by soldiers for a period of time. But in 2001 it was made a part of the Tom Yawkey Wildlife Center Heritage Preserve.

Jim didn't realize how complicated it was to gain access to the Lighthouse. Besides the local Preserve, there was the County Historical Society, and the South Carolina Historical Commission. There was even talk of bringing on an archeologist to oversee certain aspects of the investigation.

To move ahead, there was some risk. Obviously if anything was found, they probably would not be the principle recipient of any valuables found. If ever it was found out who provided the information, they no doubt would be followed and harassed.

Sarah wanted to keep everything hush hush until they could find everything out. However, it became plain they were at an impasse. There was nothing more that the flagship HMS Blackpool could tell them. Sarah was not ready to just leave the pages of history blank. They had to risk a little to gain a little. The reality though was that everything was at risk, even the property at the blueberry patch.

It was a regular work day when Sarah came into the office a bit early carrying a round box. Bringing the package into Jim's office she sat it on his desk, but he wasn't there. After a bit he came in and she could hear him say, "What's this?" Sarah got up and went back into his office.

"It's a present," she informed.

"Thank you, but it's quite unexpected," he replied.

"Open it," coaxed Sarah who was leaning up against the doorframe.

Unexpectedly, Beth beeped in on the telephone and said that Mr. Montgomery was on line two for him. Sarah threw up her hands.

"Sarah, now wait, he can wait a moment. Let's see what's in the box."

He lifted the lid off and pulled out two baseball caps. In large bold letters one read BOSS, and the other PARTNER.

Jim laughed. "Sarah, yes I do wear many hats, and I guess this is to remind me to keep them straight. Thank you for the gift."

"My pleasure," she smiled. "Positive changes are always good."

""Ah ha, you're getting after me for that conversation we had the other day," he stated.

"No, more like—reinforcement," answered Sarah.

Jim laughed and after a pause laughed again. "Sarah, Sarah, what am I going to do with you?"

Her first thought was, "Just love me." But where did that thought come from?

"Let me take this phone call, and then we better head on out," stated Jim changing the subject.

Two days passed while both of them discussed what they would and would not disclose in their presentation to the Historical Commission.

This brought up the subject in her mind that she was responsible for her share of the expenses in the partnership. Jim told her not to worry about it. If need be they would take it out of future revenue.

It was decided to present their proposal under the Hollingsworth Land Surveying letterhead to make it seem more official. Jim would represent the "client" who would remain anonymous. The client would remain an unnamed partnership. Said client would also be asking twenty percent of anything of value that was found. Hollingsworth Surveying would act as technical support through the process.

The subject of the proposal was the finding of the location or locations of the 1770 British shipwreck. The key to finding their location was linked to the North Island Lighthouse. Manifests show that the ships carried valuable cargo in their holds.

Step 1 — Find Fresnel lens device hidden in interior wall (most likely located at the Lighthouse). Proceed 70 steps up and find B & H in brickwork.

Step 2 — Attach device to existing light turret and align with a mark that looks like flower petals or a doily pattern.

Step 3 — Turn on beacon.

Step 4 — Find location where light beam strikes the ground.

Step 5 — Verify marker and excavate ship.

Two things that Jim and Sarah would not disclose at this time were the existence of a second site and the location of the flagship itself.

The following day, Sarah agreed to go to Columbia, the state capitol to the South Carolina Historical Commission to drop off their proposal. They knew it would be some days before they would hear anything back. In the meantime it was business as usual.

The next two days it rained. It wasn't uncommon during the summer to have an occasional rain event. That is what kept the coastal plain so green throughout the year.

Everyone stayed in the office and worked on indoor projects such as reducing field notes, ordering supplies, and for Sarah she was assigned to a small desk in the corner plotting survey points on a sheet of vellum.

Everything was going good until Maranda showed up. Sarah peeked at her from behind the file cabinet. "Good grief, she is here to get her hooks into Jim," thought Sarah. But what could she do? That high-pitched voice of hers could break glass. It was even hard to draw a straight line. Perhaps she could accidently trip the fire alarm. But that would mean they would have to go out into the rain. "Nope, that wouldn't go over good," she realized.

Three more days passed when Jim finally received a phone call from the State Historical Commission. They were quite interested in their proposal. They wanted to meet onsite and evaluate the proposal and locate the hidden device. If that could be found they would consider authorizing the rest. The Commission would set up a meeting that would include the Department of Natural Resources, personnel from the Preserve, and a staff archeologist that would oversee any excavating and wall removal. A boat would be chartered to take them over to North Island. Jim was asked to bring the actual detailed instructions so they could step through the process. Jim mentioned that he and one assistant would attend the meeting. That assistant was to be of course, Sarah.

Jim held a brief meeting with the whole staff to explain what was happening with this project that involved the State Historical Commission. He thought that some of them may have overheard little bits and pieces and this was to bring everyone up to speed. He was careful not to mention who the client was, and about any possible buried treasure.

Sarah thought about the last several weeks and all that she had learned, working in the field and in the office. She was learning a whole new vocabulary, giving her a new perspective on things. Whenever she drove around there was evidence everywhere of land division, property pipes, fence lines, and survey monuments. It was a whole another world out there.

She reflected on her own health as well. It had been quite some time since her last dizzy spell. Overall she felt stronger. Jim's strong work ethic seemed to be rubbing off on her. The fact was that he really had been working her hard at times. Sarah noticed the light tan in her arms from the many days she had been working out in the field.

Both of them were a little nervous as the day approached for them to meet with the Historical Commission and the Department of Natural Resources.

Sarah had four sets of the instructions printed up to hand out to those who would be attending. She wondered how all of this was going to turn out. Could these people really be trusted?

On the day of the meeting, Sarah wore a brown formal matching outfit, considering she would be representing the Company. Everyone complemented her at the office that she looked very professional.

They were to meet at the Georgetown Harbor at ten in the morning which gave Jim time to take care of other matters before they left.

On the way, Sarah got to sit in the front passenger seat and not in the back. It almost felt like a promotion in a way.

"Sarah, remember in this situation you are my assistant, responsible for historical research which is really not far from the truth," stated Jim. "I will do the talking, but I will ask your opinion when necessary."

"Yes, you'll be wearing your 'boss' hat today, so to speak," she replied.

"That is correct," confirmed Jim. "By the way you do look nice today," he complemented.

"Normally, it's inappropriate for a boss to say such things to an employee," stated Sarah.

"I was speaking to you as my partner," informed Jim.

"From my partner I will gladly accept such complements," she commented.

Jim smiled briefly, after which his thoughts lapsed back to the coming meeting. Within minutes they had covered the distance across town to the marina where boat tours would originate. Parking on Front Street they gathered their materials and walked down to the wharf. Two white pelicans circled overhead and landed in the water just out from the pier. Near the boarding ramp for the tours, they spotted a small group of people congregated. Two of them turned as they approached.

"Hello," first spoke up Jim. "I presume you are waiting for us. I'm Jim Hollingsworth and this is my assistant Sarah Bentley," he introduced.

"Yes, glad to meet you both, I'm Owen Kenton with the South Carolina Historical Commission and this is Rick Santee one of our staff archeologists, and representing the Department of Natural Resources who owns the facility is Jennifer Greer."

Mr. Kenton was moderate in height, and a bit on the slender side with dark hair and mustache, whose age must have been in the mid-forties. He had a warming smile. Rick Santee was about five foot ten in height, had light brown hair, and his age must have been approaching near fifty. Jennifer Greer stood a couple inches shorter than Rick, with long black hair, and who was noticeably a bit on the slender side. She must have been close to forty-five in age.

"Glad to meet you all," reaffirmed Jim. "I guess we need to take a boat ride to get out to the scene of the crime."

"Well, let's hope there is no criminal activity related to this," laughed Jennifer.

Owen wanted to make sure they had all the necessary instructions in hand before they left on the boat. Once that was confirmed they were directed onto a pontoon boat by the name of "Dixie Express," which was outfitted to take as many as twenty-five tourists to various points of interest along the coast.

A deck hand wearing a beanie cap threw off the mooring lines and the pilot quickly maneuvered the boat out into the channel heading south toward Winyah Bay. Sarah noticed that the pilot was a short man with greying whiskers wearing a short-brimmed hat. Attached to the boat's control panel was a microphone that was no doubt used while giving tours. Everyone found seats among the wooden bench seats that were lined up facing forward under a canvas top. Jim and Owen huddled together to talk while Jennifer Greer was pleased to start up a conversation with Sarah, the only other female onboard.

Jim was informed they would be picking up a park ranger at the South Island pier who would open up the Lighthouse for them.

Wanting to review what the specific instructions were, Jim had Sarah supply them with a copy to look over. After a minute or two Owen turned to Rick and asked him if he had brought some hand tools just in case they did have to remove some bricks. Rick thought he had it covered.

Sarah noticed all the different boats and colorful small sailing ships in their slips as they slowly made their way out of the harbor into Winyah Bay. Her discussion with Jennifer lasted for quite a while as they talked about their backgrounds and where they grew up. But Jennifer gave her an earful concerning work place stress and family problems related to her husband and children.

Sarah thought to herself, "My goodness, is this what life holds out? Maybe I should rethink this whole family thing."

Winyah Bay widened out as they motored south toward the ocean. After several miles they spotted the pier on South Island coming into view on the right-hand side of the boat. There was as expected someone waiting at the pier.

Coming aboard was Frank Dubois, one of the principle rangers on the Preserve. He was a short dark-haired man with a thin mustache. He was noticeably loaded down with all kinds of keys and gadgets.

Momentarily the boat was back on its way skirting along the east shore of South Island. Sarah's attention was drawn to a flock of white pelicans flying overhead and landing just offshore. Nearby was a family of Roseate spoonbills nestled in a group of shallow pools back in from the shoreline.

It took several minutes to motor further down the Bay and across to the east side of North Island, which was basically a long spit of land. The Lighthouse now came into view towering above the surrounding trees and vegetation. It was set back several hundred feet from the shoreline. A long pier was located closely lined up with the Lighthouse and extended some four hundred feet out into the water.

The pilot eased the throttle back and maneuvered the boat paralleling the pier. The boat attendant readied the ropes and jumped onto the landing as they slowed to a stop. He called out for everyone to use caution when using the steps leading up to the pier. Everyone stood up and steadied themselves before proceeding over to the landing platform. In single file Frank Dubois took the lead and led the group up the steps and along the pier toward the Lighthouse. Numerous birds circled overhead and flew off.

As they approached the eighty seven foot tall Lighthouse it was visibly three times higher than anything else around it. Three small utility buildings were positioned in close proximity to the round structure.

Frank unlocked a metal door in the first building. Soon he reappeared with the correct keys to unlock the main door to the Lighthouse.

"The North Island Lighthouse has been closed to the public for more than a couple of decades," stated the ranger approaching the entry door.

"Mr. Dubois, I understand this facility has been automated for quite some time, is that correct?" asked Mrs. Greer.

"Yes, since 1986, it has been on an automated cycle with a new light source," he confirmed. "The original Fresnel lens is now on display at the Georgetown Maritime Museum."

Jim and Sarah glanced at one another wondering if that was going to be a problem. Sarah looked up at the tapering cylinder of the Lighthouse seeing the glass enclosure at the top.

"Since some of you are from the Historical Commission, you might be interested in this marble plaque above the doorway that has inscribed upon it the date when the structure was rebuilt back in 1811, and the names of those who built it," informed their ranger guide.

"This Lighthouse does have quite a history behind it," agreed Mr. Kenton.

It took a moment for the ranger to unlock and open the door. Once the lights were turned on, the interior of the structure was all lit up.

"The wiring is definitely old," observed Mrs. Greer.

"The old ceramic insulators date back to 1910 when the lighthouse was first electrified," answered Mr. Dubois.

Sarah noticed the brick pattern on the inside wall confirming that this structure was indeed made up of brick. To the left was the beginning of the stone and brick staircase that spiraled upward along the inside wall all the way up to the lantern room. A black metal railing mounted on the steps decorated the stairway and gave it dimension all the way to the top.

"Well, Rick I guess this first part is in your capable hands," spoke up Owen Kenton.

"Let's see if this actually goes anywhere," replied Rick who seemed to be a little skeptical. "Well Mr. Hollingsworth, according to the information you provided us with, we need to count seventy steps and look for certain marked bricks."

"That is correct, and I'm hoping this is the real deal," confirmed Jim.

"Okay let's start counting. Everyone double check me as we go up," he requested.

Rick counted in tens, pausing to write the number on the stone step with a yellow lumber crayon. Up they climbed little by little until they arrived at the seventieth step. Rick stooped down and wrote the number on the appropriate step.

"Let's get some stronger light on the subject," he stated pulling a portable light out of his bag.

Everyone gave him plenty of room to work on the narrow stairs, scattering out further down the steps.

"Jim," spoke up Sarah putting her hand on his arm.

"What?" he asked, his voice echoing.

"I never thought about it before, but the seventy steps may correspond to the year of the wreck, 1770," she theorized.

"If this plays out, you could very well be correct," answered Jim.

"Smart girl," commented Jennifer overhearing that comment.

"I'm not seeing any letters in these bricks," reported Rick as he continued to scan the wall with his bright light. He moved further up the stairway and continued searching.

Owen clicked on a flashlight that he had brought and began checking out the section of wall below where Rick had already searched. Simultaneously, the search progressed upward and downward along the inside wall.

"This is not good," whispered Jim.

"It makes no sense. It has to be here," replied Sarah.

Digging out a small light of her own she began re-examining the area above the seventieth step.

"Where are you?" rhetorically asked Sarah as she closely examined the brick wall.

Jim ran his hand down the wall. "Some of these bricks are set vertical through this section," he noticed.

"You are so right," she realized stepping back against the metal railing.

"It's all here!" Sarah called out. "It's an interwoven pattern. Look here, it's the H. These vertical bricks form the upright segments of the letter. But notice, the right side of the H is also the backbone of the B."

"Mr. Santee, can we borrow your yellow crayon? Sarah may be on to something here," requested Jim.

Rick came back down and handed it to her. Everyone crowded around shining their lights on the wall. Sarah took the lumber crayon and began marking the wall.

"Here is the H," she drew out. A click click sound was made as Sarah drew across the grooves between the bricks. "The B is integrated into the H like so."

After a long pause, Mr. Kenton finally spoke up. "Young lady, you may have something here," he realized.

"It's possible," agreed Rick.

"Jennifer, do we have your permission to poke an exploratory hole in the wall?" asked Owen.

"Yes, as long as you don't cause the Lighthouse to fall down," she concurred.

After a brief chuckle, Rick took a couple of photos and got to work with a hammer and chisel.

"Sarah, you're going to have to come and work for me," offered Jennifer.

"Sarah, can I talk to you for a minute?" requested Jim.

"Jim, I am not considering that," she replied.

"No, this is on another subject," he clarified.

"Oh, okay," responded Sarah.

Stepping down the stairs fifteen or twenty feet gave them a degree of privacy.

"Have you ever thought about the significance of the merger of the letters H and B?" asked Jim his voice echoing.

"No-o, I guess I haven't," she replied.

"Think about it. What letter does your last name and mine start with?" he questioned.

"B and H! That's right! Do you really think there is a connection or it just coincidence?" questioned Sarah.

"Well, we are both descendants of long time British families," analyzed Jim. "And the old letter you had was addressed directly to the Bentley family; but for my side, I don't know. The Hollingsworths have been in the area for a long time also."

"This is so strange, now that you have mentioned it. How could this be? But like you say, there could be a connection that goes way back," she pondered.

Jim shook his head. "On the other hand, it may have nothing to do with us."

"I don't know, you have me thinking seriously about this," replied Sarah.

"I think there is space in behind these bricks," called out Rick. "Give me a minute and I'll have a couple more of these bricks out."

Everyone's attention was drawn back to the wall under investigation. Rick kept chiseling the mortar away around the next set of bricks to be removed. Every time he struck the chisel with a hammer blow it made a loud pinging sound. One by one they finally came loose. He shined his light back to take a look.

"There is a fair-sized cavity in the masonry wall structure, and I do believe I see something in there," he reported. "Another three or four bricks will have to be removed."

"Go ahead," approved Jennifer.

It didn't take him long to enlarge the hole in the wall with a few taps of the chisel.

"There is definitely something in there. But before we can move it, I need to take a couple of pictures of it in place," he informed.

Once that was completed he reached in and pulled out a heavy wrapped bundle.

"Let's carry this down and examine this on a table," recommended Rick.

Frank found a table on the ground level shoved up against the interior wall and dragged it out into the middle. After a couple more pictures, he proceeded to undo two straps that held the bundle together. A heavy cotton bag that showed extensive deterioration was the main covering. Inside was a copper frame with individually wrapped glass elements. Rick, one by one removed the padding to reveal a multi-lensed apparatus.

Sarah grabbed Jim's arm and whispered in his ear, "This is the real deal."

"What is this supposed to be?" asked Rick.

"A Fresnel lens device of some kind," answered Sarah.

"Well, it may have that possibility," he replied scratching his head.

"Jim, it appears that the information your client has supplied is authentic," concluded Owen.

"That would seem to be the case," he agreed. "These small feet here," pointed out Jim, "must be what fits onto the lantern devise somehow. That is if it hasn't been modified too much."

"Let's go up and see if the next steps are still feasible," replied Owen.

Everyone in single file made their way back up the staircase all the way up into the lantern room. On the way up a noise was heard down below by the doorway. Everyone assumed it was just the wind.

Through the encircling glass panes in the lantern room an amazing view was available in all directions. Georgetown was visible in the northwest and all the wetlands and groves of trees that made up the coastal plain. The curve of the earth was discernible looking out to sea disappearing about twenty five miles at the horizon.

"A lot of the original apparatus is still in place," informed Frank as they gathered around the light beacon. "From here up is the new light fixture," he motioned with his right hand.

"Can you tell me anything about these two square holes in this circular metal track, and what they were used for?" asked Rick.

"No, they have always been there, and no one ever paid much attention to them," he answered.

"Do these holes correspond to the device we found hidden in the wall?" asked Mrs. Greer.

"I believe that might be the case," answered Rick. Taking a pocket tape he measured the distance between the holes. "Yes, the apparatus should fit right into them," he confirmed.

"The other part of this is to find the alignment symbol which is a large dot in the center with radiating exclamation marks. Like a doily pattern or something," recalled Jim.

"Is this it?" wondered Mrs. Greer rubbing on a painted surface just below the metal track?

Rick bent down to take a closer look. "No-o, this one is more like a starburst or something," he determined.

A pang went through Sarah as she realized they had found the alignment symbol for the other location.

"Here it is," discovered Owen bending down. "It's been painted over numerous times."

"Yes," confirmed Rick after taking a look. "This mark is fixed, which means that the circular track should turn to align with the mark."

Rick pushed on the wide circular ring and it moved slightly. Asking for help they were able to turn it until it lined up with the mark.

"It appears that the buried ship is almost due west of us," eye-balled Jim. "The device should show us how far out."

"With your permission, Jim, let's keep all the instructions with the device downstairs for safe keeping till we can arrange to have a technician come out to run the light manually one of these evenings," proposed Mr. Kenton.

"That would be fine, as long as everything is locked up and secure," agreed Jim.

"No one should bother out here," he believed.

Sarah looked out toward the west and for a few miles there were no obstacles that would hinder the "ray of light."

Suddenly, catching her attention was movement down below on the ground level. A shadow just disappeared around one of the utility buildings to the left of the main walkway. Probably just the pilot or the deck hand wandering around while they waited for them, she thought to herself.

But one final thing bothered her. Having found the other mark there were going to be questions.

12

PIRATES

Monday of the following week, Jim received a startling phone call from Owen Kenton of the State Historical Commission.

Apparently, the day before, someone had broken into the Lighthouse and deployed the beacon and the device as they had planned to do.

Jim was quite upset and called for an immediate investigation. Owen reassured him that it was in the works. Whoever broke in had cast the device aside and had damaged it. No doubt they were hoping to prevent anyone else from using it. All the printed instructions were also found missing. He said he would call again and keep them posted.

When Sarah arrived she couldn't believe what Jim was telling her. She sat down and put her hands on her head looking down at the floor.

"Where did we go wrong?" she implored.

"You just can't trust anyone," replied Jim.

"That's exactly what the old letter said," recalled Sarah. "But we did take that risk."

"Our name was on the instructions, so it's possible whoever it was may come looking for more answers," he added.

"Our name?" she questioned.

"The business name, representing our partnership," clarified Jim.

"Yes, of course," realized Sarah.

"Were you thinking something more," he questioned.

"No, no, my mind was way off in left field somewhere," she replied.

Jim smiled as he contemplated her comment. "They're probably already aware that there are four ships in total," he reasoned. "These pirates or whatever you want to call them are no doubt still in the hunt for the others and will come looking for more clues."

"It's hard to say what they'll find if they do locate the first wreck, but either way like you say, they'll be on the hunt," agreed Sarah.

"Well, Sarah, batten down the hatches, I think we're in for a rough ride," he concluded.

"It's probably a good idea that we stay away from the berry patch for a while," she remarked.

"Despite all of this, we still have a business to run," reminded Jim.

"I'm not giving up without a fight," stated Sarah getting up.

"Just promise me you'll do nothing to put yourself at risk," he requested.

"No, not intentionally," she agreed.

Jim didn't know how things were going to work out, but felt there was going to be bumps down the road and even between them along the way.

The depressing news was on their minds the rest of the day despite the fact there was a new job to start. They had been contracted to subdivide a large tract of land into five acre parcels. First came the boundary survey and secondly a long traverse that tied in all the corners.

The Indian grass was tall as Sarah and Billy made their way through the open fields from point to point ever watchful for snakes that might be out sunning themselves, especially the infamous copperhead and the cottonmouth. In places the ground was dry and dusty. Keeping busy was a good distraction while things were playing out in the background.

When they returned to the office after a lengthy day in the field, there was a detailed message for Jim. Beth was all excited about the situation since she had to copy it all down. She read it out loud as they put their equipment away.

Owen Kenton conveyed the report that he received a call from the Georgetown County Sheriff's Department that an excavation had been discovered that appeared to reveal an old shipwreck. He had yet to go out himself and verify that, and whether it had anything to do with the 1770 treasure fleet he did not know. Owen wanted to meet him at the location south of Georgetown.

"Call him back, Beth, and confirm that we will swing by first thing in the morning," ordered Jim. "And get the exact location for us if you will."

"Sounds exciting," commented Beth as she turned to go back to her desk to make the confirming call.

"This is getting out of control," Sarah stated unhappily.

"Hang in there," he encouraged. "We still have most of the cards in our hands."

Next morning, Sarah was still feeling down about the situation. The directions took them out to an area near the North Santee River south of Georgetown. Taking Powell Road they turned south onto County Road S-22, passing a small creek called Pole Branch. After about three quarters of a mile, bright pink flagging was spotted adjacent to a narrow dirt road that led down into a thick deciduous forest. It was barely wider than the truck itself. Sarah noticed that numerous branches along the way had been broken by previous traffic. Nearly a half mile in, the trees began naturally thinning and finally other vehicles were now visible straight ahead. A clearing in the forest canopy presented itself as they drove up behind a car and truck. Trees and underbrush were visibly shoved aside to the edge of the clearing.

Getting out of the truck, Mr. Kenton was spotted with three others running caution tape around a pit that was apparently the excavation site.

"Jim and Sarah, nice to see you," greeted Owen. "But it's not under the best of circumstances."

"You're right about that," agreed Jim.

"It's definitely a ship in about the right time period," he informed. "Whoever did this took an excavator and tore right through the upper deck. But I must say, the ship's general condition shows that it must have been severely damaged when it was first abandoned."

"Any cargo left on board?" asked Sarah.

"So far nothing of significance," answered Owen scratching his head. "But we have not been able to safely view what's on the lower levels yet. But first, Archeological protocol calls for us to set up a grid on the entire wreck site. We're hoping that you'll be able to help us out on that."

"We did offer our technical support on this project," confirmed Jim. "We'll be back in the afternoon and start the lay out."

"That would be very helpful and would expedite the process," appreciated Mr. Kenton.

"Of all the years that I've been surveying, this will be the first time I've ever worked on an archeological dig," commented Billy.

"Definitely a first for me too," agreed Sarah.

"We shall return shortly as soon as we finish up on another small job," declared Jim anxious to get going.

Early afternoon they returned to lay out the grid that was broken down into ten foot increments and oriented to True North. Perimeter control points were laid out and elevations taken.

Sarah could make out the subtle depression that the ship sat in reminding her that these ships were abandoned in 'sandy hollows.'

Looking over the caution tape they could make out the large hole in the upper deck, along with a large pile of broken deck boards stacked to one side. It was then she noticed that a gravestone had been pushed into one of the debris piles. Sarah asked one of the archeological technicians about the grave marker and she was informed they as of yet had not found any evidence of a grave. The writing on the stone itself was illegible. She recalled that the instructions did mention something about a marker.

"I wonder if our client has any more information that they might be disclosing?" questioned Billy.

Jim and Sarah glanced at one another and after a pause Jim answered, "Our client has not indicated if there is anything more. We will have to wait and see."

Sarah smiled to herself, thankful that Jim was keeping a lid on the information.

Before leaving, Owen mentioned that the investigation was now moving forward, but so far there were no solid leads in the case.

He took Jim aside to talk privately so no one else could hear. Sarah wondered what that was all about, but she knew that Jim would soon update her. She just had to be patient.

Later in the day Jim revealed that Owen was considering the possibility of another shipwreck site as suggested by the other alignment mark that was found adjacent to the lantern turret. He felt too that the lens device was not damaged enough to prevent them from using it again. Jim basically told him that he would check with his client and see if there was information to back up that assumption. Jim and Sarah decided to wait before making any further disclosures.

It was pretty much a normal schedule of work the following day away from all the hubbub concerning the buried British fleet. A low pressure system was working its way up out of Georgia and by late afternoon small thunderclouds were popping up everywhere. After work Jim went over to his parent's home to visit and help out with a few chores. Sarah went straight home to help out with dinner. In the meantime stronger storm cells were developing with intermittent lightning and thunder.

Mrs. Bentley voiced her concern to her daughters about the storm and hoped that the power wouldn't go out that evening. They rushed around to get the evening meal prepared just in case that should happen, but gladly that did not take place.

Sarah looked out the window as it was getting dark watching the night sky light up from the lightning that was occurring quite some distance away. She settled into a comfortable seat and turned on a reading lamp. Forgetting about the distant storm she quickly got involved in a book she was reading. Sadie was in her bedroom playing music and her mother was going through some things in the hall closet.

A closer flash of lightning made Sarah glance out the window. Seeing something unexpected she screamed. It was the face of a man staring in at her that was briefly illuminated by the lightning.

"What's wrong?" demanded her sister coming out of her bedroom. "Not another spider?"

"No! There was someone outside the window starring in at me," she exclaimed.

"Really?" questioned Sadie.

Her mother overheard and came rushing in. "Sarah, check the back door and hit the outside lights," ordered Mrs. Bentley making her way to the front door. "Sadie, start checking the windows."

"I think he ran off after I screamed," Sarah believed looking back out the window after coming back into the front room.

"Did you get a good look at the person?" asked her mom.

"Not a good look, but enough to see that he had dark hair and a dark beard," she recalled.

I'm calling the Sheriff," decided her mother. "We've never had any trouble like this before."

Sarah wondered if this had to do with the search for the buried ships, but didn't want to bring up the subject and add to everyone's anxiety. She considered calling Jim.

Returning home later in the evening Jim discovered that his house had been broken into. Someone had forced a window open in the back. Drawers were pulled out and papers scattered all over the floor. In every room they had searched thoroughly through his belongings. It would take him a while to clean up the mess.

Somewhat angered by the intrusion, but not surprised, he considered reporting the incident, but first he wanted to call over to the Bentley residence and warn them; not to alarm them but just to be precautionary. Calling over there, Sarah answered the phone.

"Oh, I'm glad you called. Someone was outside spying on us through the window," she related.

"Just now?" asked Jim.

"Yes, several minutes ago," confirmed Sarah.

"Is everyone okay? Did you make sure all the doors were locked?" he questioned.

"We're just fine, but he sure scared the living daylights out of me," she answered. "I was sitting on the couch reading when a flash of lightning lit up the front of the house, and there he was, dark hair, and beard. His piercing eyes were transfixed right on me. I screamed and he apparently fled."

"That would be scary seeing someone staring at you like that," he agreed. "Would you like me to come over?"

"Personally, I would, but mom called the Sheriff's Department and they should be here any moment. The doors are locked and we should be okay."

"Promise me, if you do, you'll call. I can get over there in a flash," stated Jim.

"I will," agreed Sarah.

"The reason I called was to warn you, but apparently I was too late. When I got home from my parents, I found someone had broken in and turned everything upside down. Probably looking for clues about the buried ships," he explained.

Oh no," she sympathized. "We should come over an help you clean up."

101

"No, no, stay home and keep the doors locked and the outside lights on. Do whatever the deputies ask you to do," instructed Jim. "I'm going to run over to the office and check on things and post some flyers on the door and windows stating that there is no information concerning the 1770 shipwreck to be found in this office. Hopefully, that will deter them from breaking in if they haven't already."

"That might help," replied Sarah. "So, I guess I'll see you tomorrow."

Despite the mess at hand, Jim decided to drive over to the office and post the notices before he did anything else. In large bold type he printed out the notices and taped them in highly visible locations, in front and in back.

Back home he straightened up the kitchen and prepared a meal before attempting to put things back in order.

Next morning Jim came in a little early to check on the office, and initially found everything to be undisturbed. But in checking the back door he found it to be cracked opened. It appeared to have been forced. Looking around the equipment room and his office it appeared nothing was disturbed.

"Jim, you look perplexed," spoke up Beth who had just come in with Sarah.

"Someone forced open the back door," he replied. "But I don't see anything that has been touched. They must have been scared off before they could do anything."

"What? Pirates can't read?" exclaimed Beth.

"Apparently not," answered Jim a little dismayed.

"Are you going to be okay?" asked Sarah after Beth stepped away.

"I'll be fine," he answered. "What about you? You had quite a fright last night?"

"I'm okay. It was peaceful the rest of the evening," she replied.

"I would like to catch these guys red-handed," commented Jim.

"Shall we set up a trap using the second ship as bait?" suggested Sarah.

"I'm surprised you would even consider that," he replied.

"Well, the cat may be out of the bag already," she stated with some remorse.

"True, so if you do feel that way, I'll go ahead and inform Owen that we have confirmation of a second site and would like to proceed with the next phase, but with improved security this time," stated Jim

"Yes," she agreed after a thoughtful pause.

Later in the day, word came from the archeological site that the contents of the ship appeared to have been emptied a very long time ago. The so-called pirates probably recovered nothing of value.

"The plot thickens," announced Jim as Sarah came in.

"How so?" she asked.

"The Bristol had been emptied years ago it so appears," he related.

"That is now the second ship in the fleet that had its treasure removed, but to where?" commented Sarah.

"There are still two missing ships, but only one more location left to investigate," pondered Jim.

"Both ships could be at this other location as we talked about before," she recalled.

"Mr. Kenton is already aware of the second alignment mark, and will probably continue on without us if we don't stay involved," he further considered.

"I just don't want the berry patch property or the Blackpool compromised in all this," expressed Sarah.

"Let's hope it doesn't come to that before we can file the resurvey," agreed Jim.

"Better not," she strongly emphasized.

13

THE TOMBSTONES

"The pirates will no doubt continue to watch our every move," contemplated Jim.

"Which is good, if we are to set up a trap for them," commented Sarah. "But who do we trust?"

"Maybe no one," he answered. "We could set out two locations. One would be the true point marked by a 'red-head' and the other a decoy that we can set up anywhere, but logically in a place that is visible from a good distance."

"Red head?" laughed Sarah.

"Well, Yeah! Don't you know surveyors prefer red heads?" he joked.

"Oh is that so," she challenged a bit perturbed. "I thought gentleman preferred blondes."

Jim laughed. "Sarah! I'm joking. What were you and Billy painting out in the stake shed a few weeks ago?"

"Red-heads? That's right, the top of stakes were painted red," she now remembered.

"Now you have it. We'll just pound it in with only an inch or two of the stake showing," he explained.

"Should we say anything to Mr. Kenton about this?" wondered Sarah.

Jim shook his head. "I don't want to steer them wrong, but perhaps what we can do is ask them to wait a couple of days while we confirm that our calculations and field work are correct."

"Hmm, that could work, provided the pirates do take the bait in that short period of time," considered Sarah.

Finally, the day arrived for the deployment of the lighthouse beacon that would pinpoint the second location of the buried treasure fleet. Owen Kenton, Frank Dubois, and a State Marshall met Jim at the dock in the marina. There was still an hour of daylight before sunset as the boat left the harbor. Pelicans glided effortlessly paralleling their course, seemingly escorting them out of the bay. The water shimmered beneath their out-stretched wings as they flew along.

Before long they had reached the lonely old Lighthouse. It wasn't quite dark yet as they ascended the steps up to the lantern room. Owen brought the Fresnel lens in a special carrying case and set it down on the circular turret. There was no hurry as they had to wait for darkness to fully take hold.

Jim located the star alignment mark and moved the turret around to align with the mark. He next peered out along the approximate sightline and determined that it passed just north of the industrial park south of Georgetown. Using binoculars Jim was able to spot an open field just short of the main highway that would work as a starting point for the field crew.

He called Billy and Sarah on a cell phone and directed them to the open field to wait for show time. Jim considered that the distance to both locations must be very similar given that the declination of the device was fixed.

Owen had made arrangements to take the Lighthouse out of service for two hours while they re-directed the beacon to align with the Fresnel device.

Finally, darkness arrived and Frank took the beacon off of automatic, before it would normally come on and swung it around. Jim looked closely at the curved glass lenses that were sandwiched, overlapping on both sides of the apparatus. The copper frame showed some surface damage and what looked to be a small cross brace that had broken loose. Overall the damage appeared slight. Both Owen and Jim double-checked to make sure everything was lined up properly.

"I guess we're red-eye," declared Jim.

" 'pears so," agreed Owen.

Jim called Billy and Sarah once again to alert them that the beacon would shortly display itself.

"Fire it up," ordered Owen.

Frank threw the switch and a brilliant white beam emanated from the lamp and lit up the Fresnel lens. A focused shaft of light projected through the window and into the dark night.

"Wow, that is bright," commented Jim.

"They should be able to see that," observed Owen.

Jim picked up the phone to let them know that the beacon was now in operation. "Can you see it," he asked.

"Yes!" finally responded Billy after a silent moment, "but it's not very bright."

"Okay, try moving to your left, in a northerly direction and see how it changes," directed Jim.

"Will do; we'll lock up the truck and start walking," replied Billy.

Jim could hear Sarah saying something in the background. She gathered up a hand full of lathe and a flashlight to join Billy proceeding across the open field. After a thousand feet more or less it became apparent that the light was getting dimmer.

"It appears we are going the wrong way," realized Sarah.

"Apparently so," he agreed.

"Hey boss, it's starting to fade, we're reversing course and heading back the other way," reported Billy over the phone.

"Excellent, see if you can zero-in on where it gets the brightest," reminded Jim.

"We'll keep our eyes peeled," he replied.

While walking back in the stillness of the night, Sarah noticed a crescent moon appearing in the eastern sky in the general direction of the Lighthouse. She thought about Jim and a warm feeling came over her. Passing where the survey truck was parked they began noticing how the light was getting brighter. After a substantial distance the lighthouse beacon again diminished. Reversing course they came back to a point that seemed brighter, Sarah hammered in a lathe to mark that location. Proceeding further, the same illumination was consistent for some eight hundred feet. Splitting the difference they marked the center point.

Calling Jim back they reported their progress and were ready to go to the next phase. He instructed them to build a makeshift tripod out of lathe and hang a small battery powered lantern from its apex. Having completed that task they were told to walk away from the lantern keeping in line with the lighthouse beacon.

So the process began again, but in a linear direction this time. The light seemed to be brighter as they continued on out. Within a quarter mile they arrived at the edge of the main highway coming out of Georgetown. Looking across toward the west side of the road, Sarah could see a chain-link fence reminding her there was an industrial park on the opposite side.

Billy called Jim to inform him they were returning to the truck and would drive over to the sewer plant and continue their search. Sarah's heart sank realizing that if it was over there it would be very difficult to excavate. At hearing this, Jim shook his head and sighed, glancing at Owen, who was also visibly troubled by the news.

It took ten to fifteen minutes to navigate the roads to finally arrive at the main sewer plant building. Being after hours the door was locked and most of the internal lighting was off. Billy tried pushing an intercom button stating they needed to speak with someone. At least two minutes transpired before a short, dark haired man appeared and asked them what they wanted.

After a brief explanation the sewer plant operator said he would walk with them to ensure they didn't fall into a valve pit or something. Driving a short distance paralleling the main building they parked at the far end of the parking lot. Their guide quickly arrived in a quad and guided them through a maze of pipelines and butterfly valves. Billy stood up on a small platform and visually checked to see how close they were to lining up with the lighthouse beacon.

"Just a ways further," he judged. After several hundred more feet, Billy checked again. "Well, we appear to be on the proper alignment, and far as distance is concerned it would seem to fall into the building just behind us."

Sarah turned toward the plant operator. "What's inside this building and does it have a basement or anything?" she asked.

"This is where the main trunk sewer comes into the plant, and we're talking some thirty to thirty-five feet deep down to the bottom floor level," he informed.

"If that's the case, we're done here," concluded Billy. "It's a bust. I'll call Jim and let him know."

Disappointment flooded in on Sarah as she realized there was something definitely wrong. "Thank you for assisting us to check this out," she sighed thanking the man.

Upon hearing the news, Jim was quite taken back. "Owen, something is not right, we ended up in the base of the sewer plant."

"What the Sam," he commented. "Maybe the device is more damaged than we thought."

"If you'll allow me, I would like to take it back to my office and examine it more closely," requested Jim.

"Yes, but remember, it itself is a historical artifact and must be treated with the utmost care," replied Owen.

"I agree, it's a very unique object," he added.

Carefully repacking the copper framed device, they soon exited the Lighthouse and were on their way back to Georgetown.

Jim took the prized package to the office intending to just drop it off, but once inside, curiosity got the best of him. Unpacking the device he carefully set it on a flat table. The apparatus sat on its front two feet and its copper bottom frame. Beautifully formed curved lens were laid out overlapping slightly in a concave pattern. Each lens was individually held in place, top and bottom.

Borrowing a drafting lamp from a nearby table, Jim began taking a closer look at its intricate make up. He looked at the spot along the back frame that showed some damage. Grabbing the frame on both sides he tried gently tweaking it, but found it to be still rigid.

What caught his attention next was a metal piece that appeared to be partially detached. If this was a brace for the frame, perhaps this would show how far it had become bent out of shape. But, no, the end of the piece showed no evidence of it ever being connected to anything.

"Ah ha," voiced Jim.

He noticed on the bottom of the back frame two small indents. Adjacent to one of these was the smallest of images that had the appearance of a doily pattern, and the other a starburst.

"So that's it," he realized.

The metal piece was to snap into either one of the two notches, but it was slightly bent and could no longer do so. Its present position was close to the doily pattern, which made sense. Jim tried moving it over to the other setting, but it resisted at first. Suddenly, it released and shifted all the way over. At the same time all the lenses moved into a whole new configuration.

"Okay, now what?" he questioned.

For one thing Jim realized that the focal plane had shifted 15° to 20° to the right. Moving the light around he noticed that various colors began appearing on the opposite wall.

"Will you look at that," spoke up Jim.

It was a rainbow, with all the primary colors being displayed in separated bands, all in order, ROY G BIV. That's when he remembered what was written in the ship's log, "a beacon of light and a rainbow."

But what is it about the spectrum break that was a clue to the location of the buried ship or ships? One thing for sure, the pirates didn't have a clue about the second position, but as a matter of security they were not given the whole answer either.

Tomorrow is another day he thought. Yawning, he covered the device and left for home to get some sleep.

Next morning Jim found Billy, Sarah, and Carson Nash the draftsman visually scrutinizing the Fresnel devise.

"Well, Jim, you didn't tell us you were bringing it home with you," first spoke up Billy.

"No, it was an afterthought," he replied. "I wanted to see more closely what the damage was and to see if it was correctable."

"The lenses look different somehow," observed Sarah.

"They are," affirmed Jim. "Last night I discovered an alternate position that the lenses can be changed into. Watch this."

Removing Nash's drafting lamp he placed it behind the device and turned it on.

"Woo!" everyone exclaimed. Beth walked in and made a similar comment.

"A rainbow," realized Sarah.

Jim darted her a meaningful glance, which prodded a recollection on that subject, stifling any further comment. The Blackpool's log mentioned that there would be a beacon of light and a rainbow involved. There were now multiple bands of light, all different colors, that made things all the more complicated. The answer must have something to do with one or more particular colors she reasoned to herself.

"Well, what are the names of the ships that we're looking for?" asked Billy.

"Yorktown, was the very first one," recalled Sarah.

"Bristol and Andover, were couple more that we were also been made privy to," informed Jim. "Could it be that simple?" he suddenly realized. ROY G BIV?"

"Roy, who?" asked Beth.

"No!" laughed Jim. "You know, red, orange, yellow etc. etc."

"You mean 'Y' is for Yorktown, and 'B' could be for Bristol?" questioned Sarah.

"Yes, think about that for a moment," pondered Jim. "The bad guys followed the initial instructions we had, using the direct lighthouse beacon and aligning it with the doily symbol to find the Yorktown. So, last night, using the star symbol, where did that put us?" he asked.

"Probably, a good mile north of the original sightline and into the sewer plant," answered Billy.

"Correct!" responded Jim.

Taking the devise he turned it so that it was centered on the white board. Jim switched the lenses over to the original position.

"Let's pretend that the lamp is the Lighthouse," he stated. "Sarah, take a black marker and put the doily symbol at the location of the focused light."

"I see what you're doing," she realized. You're duplicating in miniature what was done at the Lighthouse."

"Yes, I want to test a theory," confirmed Jim. "I'm moving the device about 15° to the right to approximate where the star symbol pointed us to last night. Sarah, now mark the star symbol at this location on the board. Let's see what happens next."

Shifting the lenses back over, the color spectrum again returned.

"Look, the yellow is very closely matching up with the first symbol," noticed Beth.

"And the green which is at the center of the rainbow is aligning with the star symbol. There does seem to be a correlation between the two settings of the device," added Billy.

"So, if 'Y' was where the Yorktown was found, then 'B' is where the Bristol and perhaps where the other ship should be found," reasoned Sarah.

"Yes, I believe that is the correct approach," agreed Jim. "And if this is true, what we need to do is go back to the Lighthouse and go through the whole process again, but this time lining up on the blue light."

"If the angle between the 'B' line is similar to the angle of the 'Y' line, than we must be looking at a new location about a mile north of the treatment plant up by the airport thereabouts," reasoned Billy.

"Somewhere up that way," agreed Jim. "We need to keep this confidential until we can actually establish the new location," he further reminded.

"Me know nothing, noth-thing," replied Beth heading back to the front office.

"I'll reschedule our return to the Lighthouse fairly soon," informed Jim. "In the meantime we have our day jobs to take care of."

That day they stayed close to town running a short traverse around a new development that was soon to break ground. Billy could only work half a day leaving Jim and Sarah to wrap things up. It was quite breezy along the coast that morning and felt good getting back into the shelter of the survey truck. Jim made a number of notes in the field book and clapping it closed declared that this phase was done.

Jim looked over at Sarah who was sitting on the passenger side of the truck. "Well, partner, how about some lunch, my treat," he offered.

"That does sound good," she replied. "I didn't bring anything today."

"I was thinking of Sandy's Café. They make a mean burger and have a nice salad bar," he suggested.

"Yes, that would be fine," agreed Sarah.

The restaurant was just a few blocks away. The building was newly remodeled with large windows throughout the dining area and surrounded by lush green lawns. It was popular with the locals and tourists visiting the area. A booth seat allowed them a nice view of the nearby marina. A large swarm of birds was visible landing on the opposite shore.

"I don't know about you, but I'm feeling worn out. It's been a long week," shared Jim as he looked at the menu.

"There has been a lot of stress lately," commented Sarah.

"This is true," he concurred.

"How's your dad doing?" she inquired.

"Doing much better," Jim answered. "He is getting around a lot more than he has in quite a while."

"That's good," replied Sarah as she unfolded her menu.

"He thinks you are a good addition to the crew," confided Jim.

"But, Jim, a few months ago I was a mess," she reflected. "Don't you remember?"

"Sarah, that was back then," he answered. "I've been meaning to complement you and really haven't had the chance because all of the hearing ears that might misinterpret my comments. You've worked hard and have really applied yourself. And you especially impressed me with your insightfulness when we were at the Lighthouse."

"Well, thank you for that, but can I ask you something?" she asked.

"Absolutely," answered Jim.

"It almost seemed you were putting me to the test at times," wondered Sarah.

Jim smiled. "In a sense, yes. I wanted you to succeed. I saw something good in you."

She smiled back at him. "You've been kind to me in many ways, in which I'm thankful for, but you are still a man and experience has shown me that they are initially kind, then it all changes."

"I guess you'll always have that chip on your shoulder," he realized. "But for now, I'm happy to have you on the crew, and as my partner. Who knows what the future will bring."

"Jim, you're out to prove me wrong, aren't you?" stated Sarah.

"Amen," he replied. "Shall we order?"

Jim didn't say much to Sarah after their discussion at the diner. He seemed to her to be unusually quiet and pre-occupied. Nevertheless, Sarah felt she had to retain her individuality and protect herself from any future dilemmas despite the fact that things did seem to be favorable. On the other hand, she hated herself at times due to her mind and heart warring against one another.

The surveying and the drafting continued on with the Resurvey and was nearing completion. Once the map was submitted for recordation, it would no doubt be a bombshell in the community. But there was still the issue of legal access that had to be addressed as part of the package.

Early the following week arrangements were again set to manually operate the lighthouse beacon. Everything basically followed the same procedure as before expect Billy and Sarah stood by in a pull-out along the main highway near the airport. Owen was not able to be there this time, but provided the necessary security and essential personnel.

Just before sunset Jim had them fire up the beacon. Everyone was amazed at the brilliant display of color that the lenses produced once the light came on. There was no way Jim could direct them from the Lighthouse, it all had to be done from the field. He called Billy to advise them that the show had started. Billy replied they could clearly see the rainbow broken up into its differentiating colors. Blue was by far the brightest indicating they were in the general alignment of where they needed to be.

Another ten minutes was allowed to lapse as darkness completely ensued. Walking up and down besides the highway with a bright light Billy and Sarah determined that the blue was most intense further north about a quarter mile beyond the end of the airport runway. Using the top of the survey truck to stand on Billy determined that the intensity was a bit brighter the higher he stood.

Based on that, Jim plotted their position on a USGS map and drew a pencil line out into the rural countryside to the northwest of the airport. Next he gave them directions to drive on around to the opposite side, on Pennyroyal and then north on Pickeral Road to Pineberry Drive. Turning right they came to the end of the pavement and followed a dirt road for about a half mile to where the trees began opening up. From there it was just a matter of them working their way south to find the blue light once again.

With the State Marshalls following, Billy and Sarah made their way on around in the dark, reading signs and gradually making their way back into the woods on the dirt road.

During the fifteen to twenty minute wait, Jim was asked if using GPS would have been a faster way to speed up the whole process. He explained that it would not in this case, because the source information was based on direct visual sighting. It was clever what their ancestors had set in place, but it was still ground-based technology.

Soon the phone rang and Billy reported they could now see the top of the Lighthouse and a dim blue light. It was extremely dark and they didn't know what their surroundings looked like. Driving ever so slowly through an open field, they watched ever so closely for obstacles. The blue light seemed to grow brighter as they continued south. Things moved along quickly as they soon located the approximate alignment of maximum intensity. Next came the vertical component. The light appeared brighter than it had been over on the highway side. The consensus was to continue further out. In doing so they began encountering stumps and eventually ran into a dense tree line.

"Houston, we have a problem," declared Billy.

Sarah laughed. "You better call Houston then."

"Jim, we have run into a grove of trees that's blocking our continuing on this line," he reported.

"Great!" reacted Jim. "Is it possible for you to climb one of the trees and tie some flagging about where you think the brightest elevation is?"

"Yeah! I reckon, but it's not going to be easy out here in the dark," replied Billy.

"We have little choice, but to do this at night," reiterated Jim.

"Okay, I'll give it a try," he responded.

Grumbling he got out of the truck and waved to the Marshalls having them drive up behind them. With flashlight in hand, Billy walked up to a group of larger trees and selected one to climb.

"Sarah, turn on the spotlight on the driver's side and aim it up in this tree here," pointed Billy.

"Okay," she responded opening the truck door.

Stuffing a roll of orange flagging and his small flashlight in his survey vest, Billy put on a pair of work gloves, and looking back at the Lighthouse made his way to the trunk of the tree and began his climb.

Tree limbs snapped under his weight as he climbed. Sarah could hear him grumbling to himself as he worked his way up. Suddenly Billy stopped.

"I didn't sign up to climb trees. If I had I would have joined the forestry," he complained. "The light is still continuing to get brighter." Billy pushed a branch down. "Going up another few feet," he announced.

"Be careful," reminded Sarah.

By this time, Billy must have made his way up to about twenty-five feet or more above the ground.

"Well, I believe I'm seeing a slight drop off in intensity," he reported. "Coming back down a ways. "Ow! That hurt. I swear, this tree is trying to get even with me."

Billy slowly made his way back down and after taking another look decided to inch down a bit further.

"I think this is the spot, just above my head," he concluded. "I'm going to split the difference and tie the flagging between these branches."

Having accomplished that, Billy shimmied back down and dusted himself off, removing twigs and leaves from his clothing. Sarah handed him the cell phone.

"Jim, I have tied flagging about twenty feet off the ground, so that part is done," he reported.

"Good," responded Jim. "Sorry for having to make you go through that."

"Well, I didn't break my neck. So everything is good," replied Billy.

"We're almost done for tonight," continued Jim. "Take a hub and pound it in about thirty feet out from the tree and make sure it's on line. Mark it with a couple guard stakes."

In the background he could hear Sarah talking quite clearly. "Why not a couple red-heads? Oh, I would just love to pound on a couple of red heads. You hear me Jim Hollingsworth?" she exclaimed.

"Sarah-h," remarked Billy. "I think he could hear that."

"What? No way," she replied.

"I did hear that," chuckled Jim.

"What was that about?" laughed the two men who were with him.

"It's a personal joke," he explained. "She's a blonde."

"Oh-h-h," was their comical response.

"Tell Sarah she will have a chance to do that tomorrow," informed Jim.

"I can't believe I said that," she whispered to Billy. "I'm so embarrassed."

After setting the reference point Billy reported they were all done.

"Okay, that's it for tonight. I'll see you two back at the office in the morning," finalized Jim.

"Ten-four, we'll see you tomorrow," confirmed Billy.

"Well, that's it for here," informed Jim. "I'll pack up the device and we can be on our way."

"So, is there more to do?" questioned Frank.

Jim realized he had to carefully word his response. "Yes, using a little trigonometry we should be able to stake the final leg and hopefully find that buried ship."

Before leaving town the next morning, Jim stopped by at the Sheriff's Department briefly to make them aware of his plan before continuing on out to the jobsite.

"You're probably going to get on to me about that red head thing aren't you?" asked Sarah.

"No, but I do want all of us to be on the same page when it comes to setting a pirate trap. We will set the true point, but we'll also set a false point in a very visible location so it can be monitored. No one is to say a word about this to anyone else including Mr. Kenton until two days have transpired."

"So, if for some reason we are observed setting the true point, we should pretend that it's just a reference point or something," added Billy.

"Correct!" replied Jim.

No one was at the site when they arrived. The State Marshalls were probably still at breakfast.

Jim walked over to the reference hub and made sure that the backsight, which was the top of the Lighthouse, was visible from that spot.

"Looks good," he commented.

"The tree is right over here, just a bit off line," indicated Billy.

Jim glanced over at the tree. "We'll need to measure the horizontal distance to the tree and the vertical height up to the flagging to start with. If you guys will do that I'll get the theodolite set up."

"I have to climb that tree again?" complained Billy

"No," laughed Jim, "just use the fiberglass rod, but make sure you get an accurate reading."

"Good idea, I'll make that work," insisted Billy.

After Jim set up the survey instrument, he drew up a sketch of the four triangles that they would be measuring and calculating, and noted that the vertical height of the Lighthouse from the ground to the beacon was 83.5 feet."

"Sarah, take the field book and fill in the two distances you guys measured, and record the vertical angles we're about to shoot," instructed Jim.

"You trust me with the notes?" she asked surprised.

"Yes. You're up to it, aren't you?" he further questioned.

"I believe so," stated Sarah.

Jim sighted on the lantern room and focused precisely on the beacon itself, and called out two vertical angles averaging 15° 21' 20" of arc. Next he flopped the scope and sighted on the flagging tied in the tree. Billy pushed on the branches with the fiberglass rod so Jim could get a clear view. After averaging that vertical angle, he took his pocket tape and measured the height of instrument above the hub.

"You have all that?" asked Jim.

"I believe so," she answered.

"You should now have enough information to solve all four triangles," he informed.

"Working from left to right, yeah, that is a possibility," realized Sarah. "We have the vertical angle opposite side 'a' which is the height of the Lighthouse, and adding that to 90°, and subtracting the sum from 180° we have the opposite side 'b.' And using the law of the sines I'll be able to calculate the baseline and the hypotenuse."

"Wow, you're a quick learner," praised Billy.

"There is somethings that I wish she would unlearn," innuendoed Jim.

"Jim-m, my opinion is my opinion on things. You can't change that," she replied.

"Whatever you're talking about I don't have a clue," remarked Billy.

"Nothing to worry about," informed Sarah.

Grabbing a calculator, Sarah deeply sighed signaling her dissatisfaction with the subject. Solving the first triangle, she went on to solve the other three, but stopped short in realizing that there was one more step. Jim had written in under his sketch that the ground elevation was one foot higher at their location than at the Lighthouse.

"For the elevation change," she informed, "I'll just do a rise over run ratio for the final distance. And the final baseline distance is 2,089.13 feet," announced Sarah after completing her calculations.

"Very good," acknowledged Jim. "Billy, check her math if you would," he requested.

"Ten-four," he acknowledged walking over.

It wasn't long before he had checked her calculations and

found them to be within a few hundredths.

"That's great," declared Jim. "But because with all the built in inaccuracies we could still easily be off several hundred feet. So when we do our final layout, watch for anything that might be a marker or a clue."

"Don't forget we have a date with a red-head down the line also," reminded Sarah.

"Oh, that's right, you're not going to let me forget about that," he replied.

The State Marshalls and Owen Kenton soon arrived, informing them they had become briefly lost on the way over. Owen took a few minutes to look around and catch back up on what was happening.

Backsighting the Lighthouse once again, Jim was ready to move forward. Billy and Sarah cut line through the trees. Progress was at first slow. They moved ahead setting another point on line after about twenty minutes. This process went on for nearly an hour.

Breaking out into a clearing, Jim thought this would be a great location for the decoy point. About that time he noticed that Owen and the Marshalls had left. They no doubt would soon return.

"Let's hurry and shoot in the final point before they get back," ordered Jim. "Don't forget to use a red-head."

"I have my five pound hammer," declared Sarah. "I'll take care of the red head."

Billy laughed. "You're taking this a little too seriously," he commented.

"Hurry back after you set the point so we can dress up this location and make it look artificially important," added Jim.

The distance to the final point calculated out to be 497.28 feet. Bill cleared a few limbs and shrubs around the location. Sarah left the marker stake sticking out of the ground about one inch. She quickly looked around for anything unusual that might catch her eye, but nothing was apparent at that general location.

On their way back, Sarah did notice something through the

trees that did catch her attention. "Billy, look, over here on the right, it looks like a grave marker," she noticed.

"You're right, and perhaps a second one," he added.

The taller granite headstone was severely tipped forward almost to the point that it was about to fall over.

"By that, there could be more than one ship buried here," commented Billy.

"Very true," she answered. On the way back she contemplated this new discovery.

"What took you so long?" complained Jim.

"There are a couple of tombstones near where we set the point," replied Billy.

"Oh really? Was there any writing on them?" he wondered.

"Couldn't tell, one of them was near to falling over," answered Sarah.

"Hmm," considered Jim as he pulled up the instrument to set it aside. "That could very well verify that we are in the right area. But first, let us place a couple guard stakes and flag up the lathe to make this look real official."

While they were completing this and packing up, Owen and the State Marshalls returned.

"So, this is the spot," presumed Owen.

"Before I say yes, let me run through my calculations to make sure before you bring in the troops," answered Jim.

"That's fine. We won't be able to mobilize for a few days anyway," he agreed. "We'll have to find the owner of the property and go through all the legal procedure to begin excavation."

"Very good," finalized Jim. "I'll contact you in a couple of days."

"We're very appreciative of all the help you've given on this project, but do you think it would be possible to talk with your client about how they were able to acquire all this information?" inquired Owen.

"At this time, our client wants to remain completely anonymous," he answered.

14

CARNIVAL

Two days had transpired and the trap had been sprung. The Sheriff's Department monitoring the site spotted activity the previous night and moved in with several deputies to make arrests.

The antiquities thieves had moved in with digging equipment and set up a couple of portable light stands. The lighting was helpful, but when the officers moved in, they bolted and most of them fled into the woods, all except for two that were caught. Perhaps finally, some light would be shed on who these people were.

Owen Kenton was at first upset over the attempted reoccurrence, but when he found out that Jim had set a trap at a false location, that is when he really got riled up. He didn't understand why he wasn't let in on the plan, and why the County Sheriff's Department had to be involved since the State Marshalls were already assigned to provide security on the project.

Jim apologized, but just wanted him to know it wasn't anything personal. He conveyed to Owen that it was just an attempt to keep a lid on things until he could verify and hand the site off to him. Jim did wonder though about Owen's true motives. He should have been gratified that the true location had been protected and the bad guys put in jail.

In the meantime, Sarah remained in the shadows while all of this transpired. She thought it good that both of them were able to stay out of harm's way, but was still apprehensive of what the future would bring.

A property search had traced the owners to the Griggsmore Family Trust that had a current address in New Jersey. The Historical Commission was busily trying to contact the family or their attorney for permission to excavate. It was three days later that contact was finally made, but permission would not be granted till a family member visited the site to evaluate the circumstances. That date was tentatively set to take place in three days. In the meantime, materials were being gathered in a vacant warehouse offsite in anticipation of getting the needed approval.

Local newspapers couldn't get enough of the story, running a number of articles on the subject.

Jim was getting a barrage of calls to get his story since it had become known of his involvement, but he wisely diverted all inquiries to the State Historical Commission.

In one of the newspaper articles, the identity of the two men arrested was beginning to trickle in. One was a Brit hailing from an area just outside of London. The other man was from Baltimore. Both men had criminal records ranging from petty theft to grand larceny. Neither one of them would divulge any additional information. The equipment that was seized proved to be rental equipment from a nearby town. The name on the rental agreement was bogus and the deposit was paid by cash.

The County Fair was just a few days away and for the community it was an important event. In the years past, Jim's father would always buy tickets for everyone in the office, but in the last two years Jim was keeping the tradition going. Everyone was excited when he came in and began passing them out. Billy and Sarah were the last to receive their tickets as Jim made the rounds.

"Sarah, would you like to go to the Fair?" he asked handing her a ticket.

"I would love to go. I always like the exhibits and the Saturday Night Dance," she answered.

"Would you be comfortable with an escort?" he further inquired.

"Usually it is just my sister and a couple of the girls," commented Sarah. "Are you asking me out?" she asked raising her voice in realization of what he was asking.

"Yes, I thought it would be fun. Besides I thought it would be good to forget about buried ships and surveying for a day," he replied. "Don't you think?"

"That would be good," she agreed.

"I have extra tickets for your sister and mom if they want to come also," added Jim.

"Sadie probably, but I don't know about my mom. But sometimes she surprises me," pondered Sarah.

"On another matter, come tomorrow, I would like you to go out to the second shipwreck site and meet with Owen and the property owner," requested Jim.

"You won't be available tomorrow?" she asked.

"No, I have a meeting at the County Supervisor's Office and probably will not make it out in time," he informed.

"What's my official capacity at this meeting?" Sarah inquired.

"Basically, you can answer any questions that come up regarding the survey. Be sure to take notes on anything that the owner can contribute on information pertaining to the history of the property. Also, take a close look at those grave markers and see what may be written on them," instructed Jim.

"I can do that," she replied.

Sarah kept thinking about the tickets for the Fair that he gave her. Jim actually asked her out! That was significant in her mind. She actually felt happy about that, but at the same time reminded herself there could lead to pain at the end of the road.

She offered a ticket to Sadie who readily accepted it. Sarah told her that Jim was taking her out and she could tag along.

"Really?" excitedly exclaimed Sadie. "It sounds like he's getting more serious about you."

"I don't know about that, but it does sound like fun," she answered.

Making the same offer to her mother, Sarah was surprised that she too might go.

"Wow, that's great," replied Sarah.

"It's about time I get out of the house, don't you think?" she asked.

"Absolutely, yes," agreed Sarah.

"But I don't want to horn in on your and Jim's fun though," she commented.

"No, no, it's all going to be good. There's plenty of fun to go around," promised her daughter.

The next day Sarah drove out to the excavation site in her own car to find Owen and an assistant already there waiting for the arrival of the property owner. He introduced her to a short stocky young man by the name of Jared. Thereafter, Owen went off on a barrage of questions. He was curious how long she had worked with Jim's company, and how many employees there were. Then Owen began asking about the "client." He wondered if they were local or were located out of the county, or even out of the country. Sarah told him point blank that the "client" does not want to reveal themselves at this time, period. After that statement he was suddenly very quiet.

It wasn't long before a dark luxury car approached and pulled up a short distance from where they were standing. Due to the dark tinting of the windows it was impossible to see who was in the vehicle. After a moment the driver's door opened up. A tall well-dressed man got out and opened the rear door. Slowly an elderly man emerged from the backseat. He struggled to steady himself as he stood up holding a cane. When approaching the two gentlemen, Sarah could make out how the older man had dark piercing eyes and a short greying mustache.

"Mr. Griggsmore, I presume," spoke up Owen.

"Yes, and you must be Owen Kenton," he replied extending his hand out.

Owen shook his hand. "This is my assistant, Jared Dufore, and representing the land surveying company and their client is Sarah Bentley."

"Bentley?" he questioned.

"Yes, Sarah Bentley," she confirmed.

"How interesting," Mr. Griggsmore uttered under his breath. "Well, where is this buried ship supposed to be?"

"This way," pointed Sarah.

"I may be old, but I can still get around," he stated starting off at a moderate gait. "Mr. Kenton, are you from around here?"

"No," answered Owen, "I'm originally from New York."

"And you Ms. Brinley?" he asked.

"I'm from Georgetown," she answered.

"Have you considered how this may disturb the graves and the secrets of our ancestor's?" voiced the old man.

Sarah and Owen looked at each other not knowing how to respond to that remark.

"We assure you we have no intention of disturbing any graves or things of a personal nature," finally replied Owen.

"And as far as secrets are concerned," commented Sarah, "what we are uncovering here is what our ancestors left clues for us to find, and perhaps come to a better understanding of the struggles they had."

"You answered well," praised Mr. Griggsmore. "But some were traitors and some were patriots."

"I guess it all depends on whose side you were on," she commented.

"Ms. Bentley, you must be a student of history," he conjectured.

"Yes, I guess I am," responded Sarah. "In more ways than one," she kind of laughed. "My boss and I disagree on certain aspects of social history."

It wasn't long before they passed the spot where the rental equipment had been parked on the night of the arrests. But neither of them was inclined to talk about that subject. Soon they arrived at the site now marked by a couple of guard stakes surrounding the 'red-head' and a three foot lathe draped in orange flagging.

"This is the approximate location of where we would like to begin by sinking a couple of test holes, and if that doesn't work we would like to expand out from there," informed Owen.

The older gentleman looked at the stakes and then all around, as if trying to establish where he was in relation to other landmarks. Lastly, his gaze was transfixed toward the direction of grave markers.

"When I was a young boy, my brother and I used to run theses woods and we knew every secret place to hide," recalled Mr. Griggsmore.

"Then you are aware of the grave markers that are just a short way through the trees," asked Sarah motioning in that direction.

"Yes, I'm very well aware. We were told never go around them for fear that something dreadful would happen to us," he chuckled.

"Far as you know, are they real graves?" she questioned.

"I believe so. We were led to believe that was the case," he replied.

"Would it be permissible for us to take a closer look at them?" requested Sarah.

"Yes, in light of what's happening here, but don't do anything that will cause any further damage," replied Mr. Griggsmore.

"We have very strict guidelines on preservation of property," informed Owen. "That includes existing structures, cultural heritage, trees, and other ecological concerns."

"Mr. Kenton, I will sign your paperwork for this excavation, but I need eyes on this project," he declared. "Ms. Bentley, you are a local. I would like to hire you and your company to represent my interests on this project on a daily basis if you'll do it?"

Sarah put her hand on her chest in surprise. "I would have to talk with Jim Hollingsworth to see if that is possible," she replied.

"Please do," he coaxed.

Owen nodded in approval and was happy to hear the property owner's tentative approval.

"Let's go take a look at those graves," prompted Mr. Griggsmore. "I have to be heading back shortly."

It was just a short walk meandering through the trees to reach the site. Sarah stooped down and tried to read what was written on the deteriorated stones while the men continued conversing. There were partial names and dates on both of the deteriorated tombstones. Sarah gasped as she realized the last name on the right appeared to be Bentley. The other stone had a partial last name, the letters: o, r, t, h. Then the significance hit her. These were the location markers for the buried ship or ships. But this proved to be disturbing to her seeing her last name and Jim's last name buried side by side huddled together.

"Owen, Mr. Griggsmore, I could be wrong, but I believe that these are not real graves, but in reality are marking the location of the buried ship or ships," announced Sarah.

"Ms. Bentley, how can you possibly come off saying that?" asked Mr. Griggsmore a bit taken back by that statement.

"The names on the stones match clues we found at the North Island Lighthouse from which we were directed to find this place," she answered. "My suggestion is to sink a test hole further over, away from these markers. Since the ground slopes into a swale, the orientation of the buried ship probably lies in the same direction."

"Ms. Bentley, I'm impressed. You've already earned your pay," commented Mr. Griggsmore.

Owen squatted down to look at the writing on the stone markers also. "You could very well be right," seconded Mr. Kenton recalling what he had seen at the Lighthouse.

Sarah had many things to share when Jim came back in the afternoon. The whole office stopped to hear Sarah make her report of how it went at the excavation site. Any news about the project peaked everyone's interest. A round of applause spontaneously erupted. Jim sat there listening intently leaning back in his chair with feet on his desk. Afterward Jim dismissed the others to talk with her privately about the situation.

"Sarah, what am I going to do without you if I agree to this?" asked Jim rhetorically. "We do need the revenue right now to keep the business afloat. I guess Billy and I can keep up with the field work for a while. Okay! Let's do this! That is if you're agreeable."

"I'll miss going out with you and Billy; but I think this will be a good thing in the short run," considered Sarah.

"It's settled then," he finalized. "Good job Sarah. You are making yourself indispensable. Pretty soon I'll have to make you a full partner."

"Hollingsworth and Bentley, just like we saw at the Lighthouse and now again at the tombstones; united together," she commented.

"Until death do us part?" recited Jim."

"Something like that," replied Sarah. "Jim, can I speak frankly with you?" she asked lowering her voice.

"You know you can," he responded leaning forward.

"The placement of those two tombstones side by side with our names on them is disturbing to me," she confessed. "I don't want us to end up like that, because of all of this. But on the other hand, this mystery keeps calling me."

"I can understand how the sight of the grave markers would be disturbing," he remarked. "But the reality is that there are probably no remains there at all. They are just marker posts."

"Well, when you put it that way it, maybe I am taking this a little bit too far," realized Sarah.

"On another subject, are we still on for Saturday?" he asked.

"Oh, yes, I'm looking forward to it," she confirmed.

"Good, I'll pick you guys up at about ten if that's okay," questioned Jim.

"That'll be perfect," agreed Sarah.

Time flew as the day approached and suddenly the morning arrived when they would be off to the County Fair. In lieu of using his work truck Jim borrowed his parent's car to pick up his guests. It would be definitely more appropriate, comfortable, and cleaner.

Arriving at the Bentley residence he didn't have to wait too long. Half way up the sidewalk Sadie came running out declaring that the others were coming right out. Sadie was all excited whirling round and round as she made her way to the car. Sarah and her mom came out next pausing to lock the front door. Jim immediately noticed that Sarah had changed her hair. She had it braided and put up into an attractive arrangement.

"You put your hair up," he declared.

"Yes, do you like it?" she asked.

"It's quite practical. Your hair will have less of a chance of getting caught up in the branches when we're out brushing," remarked Jim.

"James Hollingsworth!" exclaimed Sarah with some surprise.

Jim laughed. "Yes, it is very becoming to you," he smiled.

"Thank you, I think," she replied.

"All board!" called out Jim opening the back door.

Seeing that Sarah was carrying an extra bag he opened up the trunk and placed it inside. After which she came around the passenger side and got in the front seat.

Getting on the way it only took about ten minutes to reach the small fairgrounds. People were streaming up to the entrance kiosk to buy tickets, but since they already had theirs it was just a matter of getting checked in at the gate.

They could immediately hear music and girls screaming on the carnival rides as they went round and round.

"Ladies, what would you like to see first?" asked Jim as they glanced at the fair program.

"The baby animals," first spoke up Sadie.

"Home economics and the botanical exhibits would be nice to see," commented Sarah.

130

"Mrs. Bentley, how about you?" he inquired.

"Well, I always enjoyed the art displays," she replied.

"What! No one wants to go to the tractor pull?" jokingly commented Jim.

"Oh-h, I'll go with you to this tractor thing," consoled Sarah.

"No, it's okay. I was just pointing out the gender difference," he chuckled. "It's all good."

"The Exhibit Hall is just down here on the right," realized Sadie looking at the map.

"I need to stash my bag with my dress in it," remembered Sarah.

"There are lockers just ahead," recalled Jim.

After finding a locker they walked over to the Exhibit Hall which featured handmade ceramics, glassware, and furniture, followed by displays of clothing, quilts, and needlework. Sarah noticed that Jim didn't have the same interest in these things, but was nevertheless impressed by the intricate work that was displayed. In another wing of the building was the arts and crafts section; and here again were exhibits that inspired them to want to try some of those projects.

Before long it was lunch time; and there was no lack of variety of food from all the different vendors that were set up along the main concourse. Boiled peanuts seemed to be a crowd favorite. Eating light they headed back over to the animal section. Sadie and Sarah both wanted to see all the baby animals.

"Jim, look how cute," declared Sarah squatting down to pet a small lamb. "Don't you just want to take one home?"

"Yeah, but after a while they do grow up," he commented.

"True, but you can still love them for a while," she stated.

Next stop was the pygmy goat pen followed by the young calves. It was after this that everyone felt the need to take a break and do something different. Sadie wanted to go on a couple of rides. Her mom went with her to buy a couple of tickets. Jim and Sarah sat on a bench in the shade just across from the carnival rides.

"Thank you for asking me out. It's been fun," reflected Sarah.

"It has," agreed Jim. "It's been nice to see and think about things besides work."

"I'm surprised Maranda hasn't called you for a date," she stated, wondering about that subject.

"Maranda has always been kind of flighty. She comes and goes. I wouldn't be surprised she'll be gone again shortly," he replied. "Don't give her another thought."

"I'm sorry, I should not be prying," realized Sarah.

"Not to worry, I really don't have any secrets to hide," shared Jim. "I guess that makes me boring. Sarah, you've worked with me for a while and I think you know me as well as anyone."

Sarah turned her head and looked at him. "Yes," she smiled. "And you've come to know me."

"Speaking of which, there is something I know you will like," he recalled.

"What?" asked Sarah dying to know what he was referring to.

"Let's catch up with your mom and Sadie and I'll take you over there," responded Jim.

After Sadie finished up with a ride, Jim led them over to the culinary section.

"Sarah, take my hand and close your eyes and I'm going to lead you over to what I want you to see," he instructed.

"Okay-y," she agreed.

Jim led her down a row of exhibits and finally stopped to turn her in the right direction. Sadie giggled.

"You may now open your eyes," he informed.

Sarah laughed. "Blueberry pies and blueberry jam, "she identified. "Well, yes, I do like blueberries." She looked at Jim kind of quizzical wondering if there was a deeper meaning in why he had brought her here. "Reflecting back, it all began at the blueberry patch, and that's where we first met," she recalled.

"Yes, that's where it all began," he concurred.

"I just hope it's all going to end well," sighed Sarah a bit weepy-eyed giving him a sideways glance.

Mrs. Bentley and Sadie both looked at him to respond to that; but he didn't realize she would react so emotionally.

"Sarah, there may be some twists and turns ahead of us, but I'm certain in the end it will all be good," Jim reassured.

"I wish I was as optimistic as you are," she remarked.

"I know what'll cheer you up," he declared, "the pig races!"

"Okay, sounds good," Sarah laughed and smiled at that thought.

After they took in the laughable antics of the pig races, Jim suggested they ride the Ferris wheel. Sarah was a little apprehensive remembering that she had a fear of great heights. He reassured her that she would be fine and he would be right there beside her. She couldn't deny that he had a stabilizing influence on her and somehow it always worked out. Sarah reluctantly agreed to go up, but with the reservation that she could bail at any time. As passengers were loaded onto the wheel and it progressively moved upward, Sarah was getting more and more anxious.

"Sarah, just breathe, you're in no danger here," reminded Jim. "Here take my hand," he ordered. "I will hold you and not let go."

Sarah smiled and interpreted that in a different way. "Is that a that promise? You will never let me go?"

Jim chuckled, "Yes!"

"Okay then," she agreed offering her hand.

Once Jim grasped her hand everything changed. She was no longer afraid. A feeling came over her that overpowered every other emotion she was having.

"Quite a view from up here," he remarked as the wheel finally began its rotation sending them to the top.

"Whew! I'm surprised how far we can see," she spoke up with a bit of nervousness still clinging to her voice.

"Look how the sun is shimmering on the ocean," pointed Jim.

"We can see all the way to North Island and the Lighthouse," observed Sarah. "Thank you for inviting me. I would never have done it on my own."

Jim smiled as he looked out over the view as the wheel descended and continued on around. They continued holding each other's hands till it was time to disembark.

"Well, this turned out to be very nice," commented Sarah stepping out onto the platform.

Sadie came running up to Sarah all excited. "Sister! Did I see you two holding hands?" she asked.

Sarah was stricken by that question. She looked at Jim then back to Sadie. "Well, yes. I was a bit anxious and Jim graciously steadied my nerves. You know I don't like heights."

"Are you sure that is all it was?" pressed her sister anxious to know.

"Sadie, your sister is telling the truth," spoke up Jim.

"Oh, I was hoping it was going to be something more," disappointedly responded Sadie.

"And what would you do if it was true?" he questioned.

"I would jump for joy," she answered.

"Why is that?" wondered Sarah.

"Because we would have a man back in the family," explained Sadie.

"Oh!" responded Sarah caught off guard by that comment. She realized her feelings concerning a serious relationship with someone else was still in a state of flux. But recently they had begun to change. Sarah smiled at Jim in connection with that thought.

From there they were off to other parts of the Fair to finish out the afternoon. After which they dined at one of the concessions and enjoyed a fried southern chicken dinner with all the fixings including corn on the cob and grits. It felt good to have a fine meal and rest up a bit enjoying casual conversation discussing the day's events.

Gradually, the sun began to set and lengthening shadows were extending themselves everywhere. With the advent of evening coming on, young people were purchasing and running around with sparklers and lighted armbands. It wouldn't be too long before the Annual Dance was to start.

Sadie went along with Sarah to help her change, but decided not to dress up herself. While the girls were gone, Mrs. Bentley took advantage of the time to talk to Jim about Sarah.

"It's good to see you two getting along so well," she started out.

"We don't agree on everything, but for the most part, yes, we do get along," he answered.

"Relationships with others have been difficult for her. Between her father leaving us and some of her past boyfriends, who were not all that nice, it has been a challenge for her," explained her mother.

"I can understand that," replied Jim. "Sarah accused me of putting her to the test by working her hard at times. I confessed that it was true, because I wanted her to succeed. I told her that 'I had seen something good in her.' "

"Well, whatever you are doing I think it is having a good effect," she praised.

It wasn't long before the girls returned in a very excited state. Sarah wore a thin cloak to protect her dress from getting dirty in the interim. She set her clothes bag down and glanced at her mom and Jim.

"What have you been talking about?" she asked.

After exchanging glances, her mother spoke up, "Our favorite subject, you."

"Oh, is that so," Sarah remarked with interest plunking down in a chair. "I'm listening," she stated preparing to defend herself.

"It's all good, Sarah," informed Jim. "I was telling your mom how good you were doing at work, and she was commenting how she has noticed a positive change in your demeanor."

"What's interesting to me," added her mother. "Is that your dizzy spells have all but disappeared. That's kind of a miracle in itself."

"Yes," agreed Sarah glancing at Jim, "I do feel better and the work has proven to be quite interesting."

"Sarah is doing so well at times," reflected Jim, "that I wonder if she will end up getting her own surveyor's license. And guess what? She is so pretty that all the business would go to her, and I would be out in the street."

"Jim!" instantly reacted Sarah reaching over to touch him on the arm. "Thank you for the flattery, but I would not do that!"

Sadie and her mom looked at each other and smiled seeing their interaction.

"Just about time to head over to the dance floor," realized Jim changing the subject.

Sarah retracted her hand realizing her spontaneous response to Jim's assertion was being observed by her family. She sank back in her seat waiting for one of them to comment, but neither of them did.

"We probably should head over that way," agreed Sarah after a moment.

"I think Sadie and I are going to go over to a glass blowing demonstration that starts in about twenty minutes," announced Mrs. Bentley getting up. "We'll be over sometime later; have fun."

"Hoping to," responded Sarah also getting up to give them a hug.

Lights were coming on everywhere as they made their way over to the open-aired dance floor. The Ferris wheel and the other revolving fair rides were brilliantly lit up with greens and reds against the darkening sky. Kids with glowing armbands and sparklers were running everywhere playing their games. It was a typical summer of warm evenings and Southern fun. Bright lights were strung out overhead the full length and breadth of the dance floor.

"You'll probably dance circles around me," believed Jim. "It's been a couple years at least."

"I'm sure you will do just fine," she commented.

The band was completing their setup including the testing of microphones and the speaker system. Many of the individuals and couples were arrayed in a wide variety of dress surrounding the dance floor waiting for the music to start. Small round tables and chairs were spotted around the perimeter. They picked one toward the middle, on the right side facing the band.

Sarah took off her cloak and set it aside on a chair and for the first time Jim could see how fancy her white dress was.

"Wow, that's one beautiful dress," he commented. "It's going to be hard to keep the boys away from you."

"Is it just the dress you think?" she asked.

"Well, no, you fill out the dress quite well," answered Jim.

"Careful boss man, you might be crossing the line," teased Sarah appreciating the complement.

A man with a husky voice began talking on the speaker system welcoming everyone to the night's featured event. After introducing himself and the band, he outlined the program that would start out first with a traditional square dance and transitioning into the slower dances. And yes cutting-in would be allowed.

To start off with, everyone lined up for the square dance and waited for the music and the first call. Jim and Sarah lined up on opposite sides from each other. Soon the music played and the first call came out starting that evening's festivities. Round and round everyone went, mingling with all the different participants. Sarah kept track of Jim's position and soon they met up as the dance progressed, smiling as they passed.

After sometime, the dance ended and everyone took a ten minute break returning to their tables.

"That definitely got the blood flowing," commented Jim seeing the rosy color in Sarah's cheeks.

"It was fun though," she responded.

Several more dances ensued, where they danced together on occasion and with others who were working the floor looking for new acquaintances. But it was later when things began to wind down, that Jim and Sarah had a chance to spend some quality time together sharing a slow dance.

After a few minutes, Sarah suddenly stopped. She was nervous as she made eye contact with him. "Jim," she started out, "do you have affection for me?"

"As you frequently remind me, it's not proper for me to say," he replied.

"Stop beating around the bush," demanded Sarah. "Do I have to quit my job for you to answer me?"

Jim smiled. "No, that will not to be necessary. Young lady, the answer to your question is, yes. I do have affection for you."

15

ABDUCTED

Tears welled up in Sarah's eyes. "I have a confession too. I have strong feelings for you also, right or wrong," she revealed reaching for him. After a long hug she wiped the tears out of her eyes. "Thank you for being my knight in shining armor and rescuing me in so many different ways."

"How could I do anything but, with such a beautiful damsel in distress," he replied.

"I'm so sorry I treated you rudely when we first met," apologized Sarah. She had a strong urge to kiss him, but did not.

Suddenly, Sarah's mom came toward them quickly across the dance floor calling their names. Sarah turned and wiped the tears out her eyes again.

"Sarah? Are you okay?" she asked.

"Yes, mom, everything is wonderful. These are tears of joy," explained her daughter.

"Really? Oh, oh, that's great," her mother finally realized. "Is Sadie here somewhere?" she asked with some concern.

"Sadie?" questioned Sarah looking around. "No, we haven't seen her. Is she missing?"

"I sent her over here about forty-five minutes ago," explained her mother. "So, you're sure you haven't seen her?"

"No. We weren't looking either, but no," confirmed Sarah.

"Perhaps she just got sidetracked by one of the amusements and lost track of the time," speculated Jim not wanting to think something worse.

"This is not like Sadie to wander off by herself like this," pondered Sarah.

"Don't panic, we can have an announcement put over the fairgrounds P.A. system, for Sadie to come and meet her family at the dance floor," recommended Jim.

"That's a good idea," considered Mrs. Bentley.

"I'll go and have the announcement made and look around at the same time," volunteered Jim.

"I'll go with you," insisted Sarah. "Mom, you stay here and watch for her."

"Okay, but don't be gone to long," she requested.

After about ten minutes she could clearly hear the announcement coming over the loud speaker system. Meanwhile, Jim and Sarah searched about half of the fairgrounds before returning. They were shocked to find that Sadie had not returned.

Sarah and her mom were beginning to think the worst and were getting emotional. Jim knew he had to do something.

"I'll get hold of the security guards and call the sheriff to get some help down here," he declared stalking off as quickly as he could go. "Just hang tight."

Jim worried that foul play might be afoot. How quickly a wonderful evening had turned bad. He was able to alert the fair security to the situation and asked if they would also contact the Sheriff's Department. They readily agreed and soon deputies arrived with a search dog.

Sarah and her mother were both in tears when he got back to them, and understandably so. Everyone needed necessary hugs.

As late as it was people were leaving in droves and only a scattered few were still making the rounds. Thirty minutes transpired when the deputies and security guards reappeared reporting that Sadie had not been located on the fairgrounds property. They were advised to go home and wait while the search went countywide.

So the all-night vigil began at the Bentley residence. Still in her dance dress, Sarah sat with Jim on the couch with his arm around her. He tried to be comforting as possible, but felt he needed to be out looking for Sadie as well. They appreciated that, but felt the need for him to be there with them.

"I can't believe how tonight has gone from one of the happiest," spoke up Sarah squeezing his hand, "to one of the scariest."

It must have been about 2:30 in the morning that they received a phone call that Sadie had been found unharmed, and was now at the Sheriff's department being questioned. Everyone jumped for joy when hearing the good news, giving each other a round of celebratory hugs.

"Let's go in my car," suggested Jim.

"I still have my dress on," remembered Sarah. "I probably should change, but what the heck, let's just go."

Arriving at the Sheriff's office they had to wait fifteen minutes till the officers had completed their questioning. When a female deputy brought her out she had the appearance of being ruffled up and frightened, but seemed to be in good health otherwise.

"Oh mom!" she exclaimed running into her arms. They hugged for the longest time.

"Are you okay?" demanded her mother.

"Yes-s, just scared half-to-death," answered Sadie.

Sadie then hugged her sister and Jim as well.

"Jim and Sarah we need to talk to you both for a few minutes in the conference room," informed the deputy.

"Really?" asked Jim as he glanced at Sarah.

"Yes, it'll just take a few minutes," she replied.

"We'll be right back," reassured Sarah.

They were escorted into the room to meet Sargent Magneson. "Just take a seat, this won't take long," he emphasized. "Sadie informs us that she was abducted by three men who were pressuring her for information on those buried ships that both of you have been involved with. They had her pretty scared. She told them about a stone building a couple of miles out of town. Does that sound familiar?" he asked.

"Yes, there is such a building," confirmed Jim.

"I stumbled upon it several months ago," informed Sarah.

"Maybe not stumbled, more like tumbled," remarked Jim.

"Jim! Please! No jokes," she replied.

"Does it have any connection with the sunken ships?" asked the Sargent.

"Yes, it does," informed Sarah.

"We'll need to go out there to verify Sadie's story," he stated.

Jim and Sarah looked at each other with long faces realizing that their secret was about to become public, besides the imminent probability that the treasure pirates may have already or will soon visit the site. Whether they additionally discovered the HMS Blackpool which was hidden below the cabin's floor was yet another question. They agreed to meet up with a couple of officers much later in the morning closer to noon.

Soon all of them were able to leave and take Sadie home where she could get some needed comfort and sleep.

"I feel so bad that my sister had to suffer because of the mystery surrounding the stone cabin," confided Sarah. "We may also end up with nothing out of this whole deal except a lot of pain and sorrow ourselves."

"These modern day pirates are playing hard ball. They will stop at nothing to get their hands on the treasure," replied Jim. "They waited till you or your sister was alone before making their move. We can't let anyone get hurt any further over this whole affair," he added after a pause.

"I totally agree," she responded. "Did we make a mistake in letting the cat out of the bag so to speak?"

"We did take a risk," sighed Jim, "but I don't think we ever thought we or our families would be put in danger."

"No," she yawned.

"We better call it a day," he realized offering her a hug.

Readily accepting the hug she replied, "Thank you for being here for us."

Neither one of them could sleep much the rest of that morning. About noon Jim drove back over to the Bentley's residence to meet up with the Sheriff's deputies. It was a calm bright sunny day with blue skies; strangely opposite of all the dreadful things that had transpired the night before. They would soon find out what damage had been done.

Jim and Sarah sat in the back seat of the squad car and directed the officers to the destination. On the way they held hands and she rested her head against his shoulder. They said little to one another on the way out.

Parking on the old dirt road near the open meadow, a couple sets of recent tire tracks were noticed in the soft ground. Apprehension grew has they made their way down through the meadow to the blueberry patch.

Jim took the lead and led them back in through the trees meandering around the large limbs and vines. Sarah noticed a lot of newly broken branches and scuff marks.

"We are here," declared Jim as they approached the stone structure.

"Talk about hidden," remarked one of the deputies.

The first thing that was noticeable was that the heavy door was swung open. The cabin was dark inside, giving no hint to what the situation was inside.

"Looks like the girl was telling the truth about this place," commented the other deputy.

" 'pears so," muttered his partner.

Pulling small flashlights from their utility belts, they turned them on and proceeded inside.

Jim and Sarah followed right in behind them. Sarah could see broken chairs, broken pottery and glass scattered everywhere on the floor. Cabinet doors were completely ripped off. Jim said nothing as he looked around in disgust.

"What a mess in here," commented one of the deputies out of the darkness.

Sarah noticed that the table was relatively untouched. She stepped over and squeezed Jim's arm signaling to him that she believed their secret had not been totally revealed.

It wasn't long before the deputies were satisfied with what they were seeing, and were ready to leave. After closing the door, they made their way through the trees and across the meadow, and finally into town. The deputies dropped them back off in front of the Bentley residence and thanked them for their cooperation.

"I guess the good news is that the so-called pirates didn't find their way down into the ship," stated Sarah.

"No, but the fall-out from this is not over yet. That property will now be under scrutiny," replied Jim. "But one thing is for sure, though."

"What?" she wondered.

"You were sure beautiful in that dress last night," he praised.

"Well thank you, that is very kind of you to say that," responded Sarah smiling.

"It might be a good idea to keep our feelings for one another to ourselves until this whole issue is settled," he recommended.

"That might be hard at times," she realized, "but given our working relationship at the office, it might be less complicated if we do keep things on ice."

Parting ways for the day there was much to contemplate concerning the stone cabin, their relationship, and her new assignment on the Griggsmore property.

On Monday, the following day, as Jim had suspected there was more fall out from Sadie's abduction. The local newspaper carried a small article at the bottom of the front page. All their names were mentioned in the article and the connection was made to the local legend of the lost ships. As cited in the Sheriff's report the kidnappers were tipped off about an old stone cabin which dated back to the colonial period, but apparently nothing of real significance was found there. The location of the cabin was not given, which made Jim happy, but it did state that there was an unclear title on the property.

Sarah came in and greeted everyone as she always did ending up at the doorway to Jim's office. Jim said good morning and handed her the newspaper.

"Oh my," she reacted.

"How's Sadie doing today," he inquired.

"Doing much better," Sarah replied as she glanced down through the article. "Can I take this with me and read it later. I need to get out to the archeological dig."

"Yes, by all means. I'll see you later," answered Jim.

Sarah quickly departed not wanting to engage anyone in conversation concerning the most recent events.

Driving out to the HMS Bristol archeological site, things were beginning to come alive. Orange safety netting was being placed to protect certain trees and the old grave site. At the same time equipment was being unloaded to begin digging the test holes. Sarah put on her safety vest and walked around and made sure everything was being protected that should be protected.

Returning to her car she sat down to read the newspaper article. Jim was right, the fall-out was coming. They could lose any advantage that they had to lay claim to the property and any treasure that was left. She was happy the mystery was being solved, but felt cheated somehow that she had lost control of solving it. Sarah took a deep breath as she watched the movement of men and equipment around the site. What did the sign in the cabin warn?—"Trust no one." Maybe that's where they went wrong she thought to herself.

Meanwhile, Jim was mulling over the necessity of hiring temporary help on the survey crew while Sarah was working at the excavation site. He interviewed a young man, a high school student who was available for two or three weeks before school started up again. Jim said he would call in a couple of days and let him know.

On day two of the ship excavation, test holes hit a wood structure six feet down in the center of the depression where

Sarah originally thought they would find the ship. It wasn't long before a hatch was found and opened up. Three members of the archeology team went below deck to assess the structural integrity of the ship and an initial view of its contents. They must have been down there thirty minutes before emerging.

Sarah was anxious to hear what they had seen, but instead they declined to say anything and went right to their vehicles to make a phone call. That made her even more curious. She made up her mind to exert her authority demanding to know what they had found.

She was told that the site was now on a security lock down. A substantial find had been discovered. A chain link fence was to be installed and armed guards were soon to arrive and provide twenty-four hour security. This arrangement was to stay in place until a full extraction of all historical items was completed. Sarah was asked to tell no one till the guards arrived in about three hours. She readily agreed looking at her watch. It would be about 6:30 that evening when they would arrive.

Sarah was excited about the news and couldn't wait to make her own phone calls. She thought about Jim and their relationship and felt a warm glow come over her. It would be nice to share some good news with him in view of all the negative things that had happened of late.

Two hours later two trucks arrived towing portable lights, and soon thereafter bigger trucks loaded with fencing materials pulled in. After another thirty minutes, workers to install the fencing showed up, and not too far behind them came the security guards.

Sarah felt she could leave now that everything appeared to be secure for the night, besides the fact that she was getting quite hungry. About an hour later Sarah made a call to the property owner and to Jim giving them the good news.

Jim was overjoyed to hear that something of value was finally being found after all their effort. He could hear the excitement in her voice and was happy that there was something positive to displace the recent tragedy. But there was bad news that he did not want to share with her. Jim wanted to preserve her joy for as long as he could.

Sarah went out to the job site directly the next morning to see what progress had been made over night. The chain link enclosure was nearly complete and the archeological crew was preparing for the day's work. Security guards kept a constant vigil on everyone coming and going. She was immediately granted access in and out as she pleased. It was made known that nothing would be removed from the ship till the following day, until the first items could be catalogued, photographed, and measured.

At noon time, Sarah made her way to the office to check in and see what was happening. She got to meet, Dan, who would be temporally filling in on the survey crew. It was surprising to her how quickly she had been replaced.

"Hope everything is still going good at the excavation site," stated Jim offering her a chair across from his desk.

"Everything is moving right along. The security fence went up overnight and there are guards on duty," she answered.

"Well, I'm glad it's all going good," he commented. "Sarah, there is one thing though that's got me a little nervous," he confided.

"What now?" wondered Sarah.

"Another survey crew was spotted in around the blueberry patch property yesterday, and from my contacts at the Courthouse I've learned that two individuals, from out of town are searching the records in around that area as well," he disclosed.

"Oh, wow. Does that mean someone has found out about the hiatus?" she speculated.

"Perhaps, but it's more likely they have only learned about how the title to the property is unclear," answered Jim. "It may be their way of finding a way to legally dig on the property, now that the location is now under public scrutiny."

"We're going to ultimately lose everything!" emotionally responded Sarah.

147

"Well, the good thing is we are way ahead of them, but we're still lacking legal access," he reminded.

"What if no one can acquire legal access?" she questioned.

"It would remain in limbo, until probably one of the adjoining properties would file on it and it would be merged with their property," explained Jim.

"Umm, that would seem to preclude the adjoining properties from granting access to anyone so that they could eventually acquire it for themselves," reasoned Sarah.

"Sarah," he whispered, "you are not only pretty, but you are also so very smart." Returning to a normal voice, he commented further, "That could very well be the case."

"Thank you, but can things get any worse?" she wondered. Sarah stood up and leaned across his desk and whispered, "It almost seems that ever since the dance the other night, everything has gone wrong. Maybe we weren't meant to be together."

"You don't really believe that do you?" he questioned.

16

FULL DISCLOSURE

Before Sarah could respond, Beth buzzed in saying that Owen Kenton was here to see him, effectively interrupting their private conversation. Jim replied he would be right out.

"Sarah! Think about what's really important will you?" he requested getting up.

Leaving his office, she went to her work station to fill out a daily report. She sighed thinking about Jim's retort. Her back was turned as Owen followed Jim to his office.

Whatever Owen came to discuss with Jim sounded serious. She could only hear a word here and there. Mention was made of the kidnapping and the stone cabin. At some point Sarah over heard the word, lawsuit. That got her attention. Getting up she stepped over closer to the doorway. Owen mentioned something about the National Antiquities Act and how there could be prison time for anyone withholding information. A couple of sentences later Owen raised his voice a bit louder, saying he would take Jim, his company, and his client to court if full disclosure was not made. Even if it came out later that they were hiding something, he would be dealt with judicially. There was a long silence. Sarah thought she better step in and intercede. Before she could do so, she heard Jim say there was one location that has not yet been disclosed.

Sarah felt like lightning had struck her. Stepping into his office she glared at him. "How could you do that?" she protested.

Owen was startled by her sudden appearance and exclamation. He turned to see her standing in the doorway.

"Sarah, we don't have much of a choice," replied Jim.

She stormed out of the office in a huff. Everyone working up front heard that outburst and wondered what had happened.

"I'm sorry if I've created a rift between you and Sarah, but we need a complete revelation on this matter," spoke up Owen.

Beth came in quite concerned about Sarah. Jim explained there was a legal entanglement with one of the archeological sites and Sarah was rightly frustrated. And he frankly did not know how this was going to end.

Soon Jim was left alone to deal with all the fall-out and this latest event. Basically, they were left with nothing, after all the work they had put into it. He also agreed to take Owen and his archeology crew out to the stone cabin in a day or two.

Meanwhile, Sarah felt betrayed and didn't know what to do, but cry. Eventually she made her way home. Her mother noticed she was home early and had been crying.

"Sarah, what happened?" she wondered.

"Men cannot be trusted!" declared Sarah. "Jim is no different than the rest of them."

"Why, what happened?" again quizzed her mother.

"He revealed to Owen with the Historical Commission the location of the final ship that we were keeping secret," she explained. "He should have talked with me first. We were supposed to be partners in this deal."

"He must have good reason to break confidentiality," felt her mom.

"Owen threatened lawsuit, based on some Antiquities Act if any information about the shipwrecks was held back," recollected Sarah.

"It sounds like he was trying to protect you and him," she replied.

"Maybe, but he didn't take the time to consult with me first," reiterated Sarah.

"It's like a husband and wife relationship. There are times you will need to forgive," explained her mother.

"Like you forgave dad?" Sarah retorted.

"It's not the same. I didn't forgive your dad because he didn't care anymore," she replied. "He didn't want to be part of our lives any further."

"I frankly don't want to talk about it anymore," finally stated Sarah.

"I have only one final thing to say," concluded her mother. "If you can't learn to forgive, you're not ready to move on with the rest of your life."

Reviewing the Resurvey Jim realized that it was almost complete. There were a couple of minor errors to correct and a Certificate of Access to add, which would include the book and page in the Official Records where the legal access to the property was recorded. But with everything that had happened recently he wondered if it was even worth pursuing. It would be so easy just to let someone else fight it out. At least there was the value of the land, besides the fact that he had already spent considerable time and energy to do the survey and draw the maps.

He needed to talk with the adjacent land owners, and see if anyone was agreeable. That included the property he had just completed a survey on a few weeks before. The very one that he was working on when he first met Sarah and her sister.

Jim tried calling Sarah on her phone, but she would not pick up. He tried calling her at home, but Mrs. Bentley answered and said Sarah would not talk to him, but she would be out at her job in the morning. Jim thought that it was a good sign that she hadn't completely given up.

Next morning he stopped by the project site on their way to their next survey job along with Billy and Dan. Jim wanted to see if Sarah was there and to speak to her, besides checking on the progress of the artifact retrievable. Billy first spotted her

151

standing just inside the chain link enclosure taking notes on items being made ready for transport.

Jim also noticed that Owen Kenton was onsite also. He really didn't want to speak with him, but soon as Jim stepped out of the truck he immediately came over.

"Glad you came by," greeted Owen who seemed to be trying to keep things on a friendly basis.

"I need to check on Sarah and see how things are going," replied Jim.

"Yes," he acknowledged. "I tried talking with her earlier, but she wouldn't give me the time of day. No one really understands how much both you and Sarah have been an integral part of this project."

"If I apologize, it might help," believed Jim.

"On another subject, we need to get together and see this other location," reminded Owen.

"I guess we can't hold off the inevitable forever," he commented. "How about Saturday at nine in the morning, would that work?"

"I could make that work," agreed Owen shaking his hand.

"If I can get Sarah to talk to me, I would like her to be involved," added Jim.

"Whatever you want to do," he replied. "Just to let you know there has been some significant discoveries made here already. Large quantities of silver and gold coins are being brought up as we speak."

"Wow, I guess the local legend about there being a treasure aboard these ships was absolutely true," commented Jim.

"This may be the most significant archeological find in this state for quite some time," added Owen.

Seeing Sarah step out of the enclosure, Jim excused himself to go speak with her. Seeing his approach, she folded her arms around the clipboard and held it against her chest.

"Looking up at him, she first spoke. "Jim, I have nothing to say to you."

"Sarah, I want to apologize for jumping ahead without talking to you first," he stated.

"Umm," she considered, "apology is good, but I have a feeling this could happen over and over again."

"I'm not perfect. As hard as I try, I'll never be perfect," conceded Jim.

"At least you're honest in that," replied Sarah.

"May I ask you if you would be willing to guide Owen and his associates over to the stone cabin?" he asked.

"I really, really, do not want to do that," she answered. "That property is special to me, and I thought it was to you also."

"It is, but we can't hide its historical content forever," reasoned Jim. "I won't go and bother you with my presence, but you can disclose whatever you want to them. If you don't want to show them what's below the floor, we can plead ignorance."

Sarah took a deep breath. "It is true that the cabin has become known. Yes, I will take them over there and consider the rest."

"Thank you," praised Jim.

Turning, he headed back to where Billy and Dan were waiting for him. Back on the road they headed off to their next jobsite.

Sarah watched him go. It felt like a page in the book of her life had just turned. She could feel a dramatic difference in their relationship. That spark didn't seem to be there anymore, and it hurt.

Next day, Jim talked with two of the land owners surrounding the blueberry patch to no avail. This was disappointing. He could feel things closing in on him with no way out.

Sarah remembered the log book of the HMS Blackpool that she had hidden away. It would have to be surrendered if she decided to show them the buried ship. All the instructions and the clues to the Lighthouse that led them to the other ship locations were all there.

On Saturday morning, Sarah met Owen and two of his team at East Bay Park. They followed her along the back roads to arrive at the parking spot by the meadow. Having brought the HMS Blackpool log book she slid it under the front seat for safe keeping, and then locked the door.

"We'll need lights, it's dark in there," she informed opening up the truck lid of her car.

"Is it far?" asked Owen.

"Not too far; down through the meadow and into the trees," pointed Sarah.

Leading them down through the meadow, she still pondered whether to show them the buried remains of HMS Blackpool. Keeping it a secret could lessen the complications of them acquiring the property. But on the other hand there could be lingering legal issues if they withheld information related to a maritime archeological feature.

Approaching the berry patch, Sarah looked for the first stepping stone. She had no intention of revealing who made the discovery and when.

"This is one of a number of stepping stones that leads back to the stone cabin," pointed out Sarah.

"Interesting," spoke up one of Owen's assistants, "the track of a lion."

"Yes, now follow me through the trees and watch your step," she coaxed.

"Thick as a jungle in here," commented Owen as they slowly worked their way back in.

"Here we are," announced Sarah stepping into the clearing that Jim had cut with the chainsaw.

The old weathered door was still closed as they had left it. The three men were astonished at the sight of the stone structure wrapped in the forest foliage.

"Anchor chain!" discovered one of the assistants.

"This place was barricaded like Fort Knox," she commented.

"Can we go inside?" asked Owen.

"Yes," affirmatively answered Sarah, "just help me shove this door open."

Once the door was open, lights came on and without hesitation the anxious visitors stepped inside.

"Watch where you step," warned Sarah. "There's broken stuff all over the floor. The crooks in their haste broke up the whole place."

"Oh my," someone spoke up out of the darkness. "These were all period items, the chairs, the pottery, and the table."

The investigative team searched through all of the shelves and cupboards, and throughout the room muttering to themselves. After a few minutes the excitement began to wane.

"Must have been a meeting place of some sort," concluded Owen.

"This table is fixed in place," noticed one of the other men.

A pang ran through her, as she was reminded there was an important decision that she had to make.

"Some of the chairs and the pottery should be able to be restored," believed one of Owen's assistants.

"Sarah, I don't see anything here for you to have gotten so upset about," remarked Owen.

Sarah took a deep breath. "Because there is more to see," she declared.

"Really?" he questioned.

"Yes!" she confirmed. "Stand back from the table while I unhinge it."

Sarah pulled the finials out and began to lift the table up. Asking for help the table continued to tilt up and the floor began to open up as it had in the past.

"This is incredible, a secret hatch," realized Owen. "How did you discover this?"

She didn't answer. "Follow me down, and watch your head. There's a low cross beam right under here."

Sarah stepped down into the dark environs. Their footsteps echoed as they made their way down the crude stairs. Passing through the second floor the foursome came to the bottom of the stairway. She shined her light first in one direction in the hallway then in the other.

"Welcome to the HMS Blackpool, that at one time served the clandestine interests of the British empire," introduced Sarah.

"I'm impressed, Sarah," praised Mr. Kenton. "This is now the third ship out of the fleet."

"You will not find any gold or silver aboard this ship, just firearms, uniforms, cannons, and other miscellaneous supplies," she further informed.

"Why? Did you already remove them?" questioned one of the men.

"No, there was nothing here to begin with. If there had been anything, it probably was moved to another ship such as the Bristol, or to another place," answered Sarah.

The team scattered searching through the ship examining its contents and layout. Sarah overheard one of them comment that this ship was similar to the other one, but bigger. Finding their way down into the great room they found evidence that this was indeed the HMS Blackpool. She now wished that Jim was here with her. After some time, and a lot of whispering in the darkness they returned to the stairs ready to go back up.

At that point a noise was heard up above. Racing up the steps and into the cabin they glimpsed someone making their way through the trees trying to get away.

"It appears someone has followed us here," realized Owen. "We better post a guard or two over here also, same as we had to do at the other site."

After lowering the table and closing the floor back up, they shoved the door closed and headed back to the vehicles.

"I have one more thing for you in the car that you'll find to be very enlightening," stated Sarah. Going to her car she retrieved the log book. "Here is the log book of the HMS Blackpool. You'll find contained herein the instructions that had been followed to find the other two ships and a complete manifest of the entire fleet. On a personal note, you'll find that we have not held anything back."

"Is your client in agreement with this," he asked.

"The client is reluctantly in agreement," she answered.

"Sarah, thank you for coming forward on this, and for Jim's cooperation also. It's best that you did this for everyone concerned," stated Owen.

"I guess," Sarah replied.

"This particular ship doesn't have the same content as the one we're working on now, but it does have a lot of historical artifacts," he commented.

"There is a lot of history bound up with this ship," she agreed.

"There is still one more ship to account for. I'm thinking we need to do more test holes adjacent to the present excavation," considered Owen.

"Interestingly, there are two grave markers at that site which could be indicative that there may be two ships buried at that location," concurred Sarah.

The investigative team soon left leaving her standing there alone. Looking back toward the berry patch, she was struck with the realization that everything was now gone, the mystery, the hope to find a treasure, and probably no chance to acquire the property itself. All there was now was her assignment at the Griggsmore property, and a busted relationship with Jim. That was depressing.

17

THE PROPOSAL

Come Monday, Owen ordered more test holes to be dug adjacent to the HMS Bristol excavation. It would be another three days before that particular crew could return. Meanwhile, the extraction of valuable and historical objects continued to stream out of the belly of the ship. The integrity of the hull on this vessel was far superior to that of the other two ships. Owen wondered if all of the monetary treasure was stashed aboard this particular ship or was it also distributed to the yet to be found, HMS Andover, which could be right next to it.

Sarah faithfully stayed right with the progress of the project day after day. She only stopped at the office to drop off daily progress reports. Jim was never there. Beth was as usual always concerned about her and how she was doing.

Owen made an appointment with Jim later in the week to discuss the legal status of the land that surrounded the HMS Blackpool and the stone cabin. Because of the hiatus and the uncertain character of the property, Owen decided to speak with the State Attorney General's office about how to gain the authority to begin archeological work at that site. The good weather would only hold out for another month and a half before the seasonal rains would return.

Sarah learned from the crew working onsite that the British Government had filed a claim concerning the 1770 fleet with the United States State Department. Who in turn turned it over to the Justice Department for review. It was amazing to her that this whole thing had gone global. There was little chance she or Jim would ever see any profit from the discovery.

About noon, the call came in that the guards stationed over at the stone cabin had been taken by surprise by a number of masked men. They tied them up and proceeded to break through the floor of the cabin with sledgehammers. After spending some time in the bowels of the ship they left with arm loads of firearms and other items. Finally, one of the guards got loose from his bindings, freed his partner and called for help.

Sarah wasted no time in getting over there to see what kind of damage had been done. The guards had a travel trailer set up in the meadow just out from the blueberry patch. County Sheriff deputies were now onsite questioning the guards. A number of people were talking in a group and a couple of stragglers were coming out of the trees from the cabin.

No one paid attention to her as she made her way back into the cabin. The pathway had become quite trodden down from what it was originally. Reaching the door Sarah could see the great hole busted in the floor. She carefully stepped her way around and made it over to the top of the descending stairway despite the missing floorboards. Clicking on her light Sarah descended. Reaching the next level she quickly traveled down the hallway, one way then the other. Many of the firearms were missing as reported, and a small number of British uniforms had also been removed. Obviously, the bigger items such as the cannons and the ammunition racks were not touched. Further down, nothing in the great room seemed to have been bothered either.

Sarah thought about this ship that sailed the seas in its glory days. Now it was but a tomb and grave robbers were knocking on the door.

Back in the meadow near the guard's trailer, two technicians from the other site saw her come out and questioned her on what seemed to be missing. After giving the information to them and subsequently to the deputies, a call came in that someone was trying to make entry onto the HMS Bristol site.

The Sheriff's Department quickly sped off to confront this new dilemma. Sarah and the other technicians were told to hold tight before trying to come back over. Twenty minutes later they were informed it was safe to return to the project site.

On arrival they found out that someone had cut a hole in the back fence and had gained entry, but it appeared they had been scared off before getting to anything important. The desperados were now getting more desperate. They used the incident at the blueberry patch to provide a distraction so they could move in on the other operation as well.

The fact was that nearly two million dollars of treasure and artifacts had already been transported offsite by armor truck and caravan, with more to come.

During the week Jim with the rest of the survey crew worked on a parcel of land in the far southwest corner of the County. Coming and going he glimpsed the out-of-town survey company working in and around the south side of Georgetown, which reminded him that the rival company was no doubt quickly catching up with him to claim the property. The problem was still legal access. He had to talk with the other surrounding land owners. One of whom was a relative and a recent client. Jim was reluctant to ask a favor from a relative, but it might come down to that.

The land owner on the south side had become privy to the land dispute and wouldn't budge an inch.

Jim next approached his elderly aunt with the request for an access easement along the edge of her property. She was unsure and indifferent; despite the fact he had surveyed her property, and was now offering her money for the easement. Her husband had passed away some years before, and she now lived alone and had become more or less a recluse. She told Jim she would think about it.

What more could he do? There was nothing that the others who were also pursuing the same course of action could do was there? Perhaps they had deep pockets and could offer the land owners a lot more money.

The Historical Commission's appeal to the Attorney General's office received some immediate attention. They received temporary control over the site until such time that the archeological recovery work had been completed.

Owen and his group wasted no time and immediately brought in a second crew and assigned them the HMS Blackpool. It was decided early on that due to the poor condition of the hull of the ship nothing would be done to preserve it or excavate it. Because of the superior condition of the HMS Bristol, it would be the only one that was deemed recoverable.

Test holes dug adjacent to the HMS Bristol hit wood decking at about eight feet down. The consensus was that they did find the other ship, the HMS Andover. It would have to wait until the work was complete on the HMS Blackpool.

Owen didn't want to keep two operations going for long so he decided to expedite the Blackpool operation and refocus back on the Bristol. The second crew made quick work of documenting, removing, and transporting all of its historical contents. Within five days the job was done, and the Blackpool became just a black hole in the ground.

Sarah was sad to see all this come to pass. It left her feeling empty as well. The mystery and the treasure was all transitory. She missed Jim more every day and realized that she needed to swallow her pride and do something about it. She came up with a plan that seemed risky and a bit bold, but felt it was the right thing to do. Sarah decided to order another hat or two as she had done in the past. Sarah realized that he was her real treasure. The only question now was: how did he feel about her?

Opening the mail, Jim received a letter from the State of South Carolina Historical Commission. Written in legal language it laid out the fact that the State of South Carolina has disclaimed any future interest in the property described herein. That was good news. It cleared away one obstacle to the acquisition of the berry patch property.

Jim didn't have to wait long until the other shoe fell. He received a phone call concerning the other formable issue, namely legal access. His aunt wanted to see him face to face to talk about it.

After work he went over there to see what she had in mind. Apparently his parents had talked with her about what was going on, including that which involved Sarah. The proposal she made included Sarah, and it was the only way she would grant an easement across her property. Jim was stunned and speechless. He shook his head and indicated that he may not be able to make it happen. She told Jim if you want this to work, you'll make it happen. His aunt told him she was interested in helping the next generation get rooted. He thanked her, and said he would try to make it fly.

Getting up to leave he noticed something on the wall that caught his eye. It was a large ornate key displayed in a small glassed picture frame.

"What do you know about this old key?" he inquired bending over to take a closer look.

"It's been in the family for a very long time, and I understand that it had an important purpose, but no one now knows what that was," she replied.

"I know exactly what this key goes to," informed Jim. "Have you ever noticed the decorative H on the key?" he asked.

"Yes, but I haven't really looked at it in years," confessed his aunt.

"There were two keys, one designated by a B, and the other with a H. Both were to be used together," informed Jim.

"And what did they go to?" she asked.

"Possibly the treasure that is associated with the 1770 scuttled British fleet," he revealed.

"James Hollingsworth, I believe you are absolutely correct!" spoke up his aunt. "Go, take it. But it has to stay within the family."

"I will do just that," he excitedly agreed.

Driving back, he considered the significance of finding the second key and the proposal his aunt laid on him. He also thought about the seriousness of his relationship with Sarah, and whether it was still practical to pursue the land that had been resurveyed. In his heart he knew what the answer was to both. The next step was to confront her with the proposal. She hadn't talked to him in days, and maybe she wouldn't.

Two days later Sarah came into the office carrying a round box. But before coming in she decided to remove one of the hats she had ordered, feeling that it didn't really convey how she felt. Everyone in the front office was happy to see her. She took a couple of minutes conversing with the girls before heading back to Jim's office.

"Hi," Sarah spoke sticking her head in the doorway.

"Sarah! Good to see you. You were making yourself a stranger," greeted Jim.

"I hope you will forgive me for going off on you the other day," she apologized as she sat down in the chair opposite his desk.

"Of course I do," he firmly answered. "I have a proposal for you, and I don't know if you'll seriously consider it."

"Proposal?" questioned Sarah.

"Yes, but this is kind of usual how this has all come about," partially answered Jim.

Sarah had kind of a quizzical look on her face. "Jim, what are you talking about?"

"I've been speaking with the adjoining land owners around the berry patch concerning legal access," he started out.

"Oh! How is that going?" she asked.

"I found one property owner to agree," replied Jim.

"Wow! Who was it?" asked Sarah.

"I'll tell you momentarily, but there is a catch to this deal," he revealed.

"And what would that be?" she demanded feeling a little frustrated wanting to get to the bottom of this.

"In order to receive the easement to the property, we, you and I, have to get married," explained Jim.

"Married?" she questioned in almost disbelief.

"My aunt owns the land that I was surveying when we first met," he further explained. "Apparently, my parents talked to her about what has been going on, and boom! This is what they concocted."

"Are you seriously considering this?" asked Sarah.

"Yes!" was his firm answer.

She looked at him. "You would marry me with all my problems?"

"Yes, I would," smiled Jim.

Sarah took a deep breath and clutched the box in her lap. "Wow, this is huge," she stated.

"It is," he agreed.

After a long pause, she stood up and placed the box in front of him. "Here is my answer, open it."

Jim took the lid off to see a brand new cap inside. The label on the front spelled out the word: HUSBAND.

"Did you special order this just for me?" asked Jim.

"Yes," responded Sarah smiling. "I miss you. I want you to be a part of my life."

"It seems we are like-minded on this matter," he concluded. "Well, you know what the next step has to be. I need to make this official and propose to you."

"You can, right now if you like," she suggested.

"Okay, then," agreed Jim holding his hand out across the desk. She reached over to grasp his. "Sarah Bentley, will you of your own free will, please be my wife."

"Yes, I will!" Sarah soundly answered a bit weepy eyed. "But I don't have a ring on my finger yet," she pointed out.

Jim froze, thinking what to do. Then he looked at his hand and pulled a ring off of his own finger. "Here," he responded. "This will work until I can get the real thing." Slipping the ring on her finger he could tell it was a little large for her.

"This will work for now," she agreed admiringly looking at it.

"Can I kiss the bride to be?" asked Jim.

"Here in the office?" wondered Sarah looking around.

"Yes!" came the answer from the other room. It was Beth.

"There's your answer," he responded.

Getting up he came around the desk to embrace and kiss her. Afterwards they remained in a hug for the longest time.

"I feel so safe in your arms that I don't want to let go," she confessed.

Everyone in the office was now standing in the doorway or just outside smiling, cheering, and clapping. Beth was drying her eyes.

Sarah turned and displayed her engagement ring and said: "Yea!"

"Okay, everyone back to work," ordered Jim. "We'll keep you all informed."

"Wait till my mom and sister hear about this," realized Sarah. "I will probably have to peel them off the ceiling."

"You're probably right about that," he laughed.

"I do want to make one thing clear, my dear future husband, that I'm not marrying you to acquire the berry patch property, but it's because I love you. You are my treasure," she explained.

"Wow, that's the most beautiful thing that I think that I've ever heard," replied Jim. "I agree. After all the work that we've done together there's no guarantee we'll see success, but we'll always have each other."

On the way home she thought about all the twists and turns in her recent life that had led up to this moment. It was amazing to think about this amazing change of circumstances. Was this a hurried decision to marry Jim? Was this the right thing to do? In her mind and heart she knew it was.

Sarah was unsure how to drop this bombshell on her family, but figured however it came out it would be good.

"I'm home," announced Sarah closing the front door.

"Good to hear," answered her mom from the living room.

Sarah put her stuff down on the dining room table with no one paying any attention to her.

"I won't be living here much longer," she suddenly announced.

Her mother dropped the book she was reading with a perplexed look on her face. Sadie also had the strangest look on her face that said: 'what's wrong with you?'

"What are you talking about?" her mother demanded.

"I'm engaged to be married," she explained.

"You're not for real are you?" disbelieved her sister.

Sarah displayed her ring, letting it speak for itself.

"Oh my!" shrieked Sadie jumping up.

Her mother placed her hands on her cheeks in surprise as it sunk in.

"Let me look at that ring," her sister requested.

"This is not an engagement ring," stated Sadie.

"No, but it will do until we can get the real thing," explained Sarah.

"Sarah! Stop beating around the bush, who are you engaged to?" asked her mother feeling frustrated.

"You know the young fella down at the corner grocery store that does the bagging," she teased.

"You're fooling me," was her mom's response.

"I am," confessed Sarah laughing. "It's Jim, Jim Hollingsworth, who do you think?"

"Well, that's more like it!" she approvingly replied.

"Yeah! I just knew it was going to happen!" excitedly exclaimed her sister. "But, how did this come about? You weren't even talking with him," she reminded.

"Well, I think the problem was mostly me," confessed Sarah. "As you know I can get stubborn about things at times."

"That's the truth," replied Sadie.

166

"Anyway, as you know, I was quite upset over the issue concerning the buried ship. But, in the end I also decided it would be best in the long run to let it go. I felt bad. I felt distant from Jim and as the days piled on, I realized that I was painfully missing him. So, I figured that I needed to set things straight between us."

"You apologized?" wondered her mother.

"I did!" she answered. "But, before I could say anything more, he goes and makes me a proposal."

"A proposal? Is that the same as being proposed to?" asked her mom.

"In this case, it was," answered Sarah

"This sounds more like a business arrangement to me," she commented.

"No, it really isn't. Jim's aunt offered us an easement to acquire the berry patch property—if we got married. But the truth of the matter is, we wanted to get married anyway. It's all good."

"Wow, how interesting," remarked her mother.

"Have you set a date yet?" curiously asked Sadie.

"No, we haven't had a chance to figure anything out yet," realized Sarah.

"You will, that's one of the initial joys of marriage," responded her mother.

"I'm still reeling at the turn of events today," she conceded.

"This will be a big change for you and a change for us too," realized her mom.

"Yes, but I'm thinking it will be a good thing for all of us in the end," believed Sarah.

"I think so too," agreed Sadie. "I'm very happy for you."

"Thank you," she replied.

A round of hugs ensued and a few tears of joy. It took Sarah a while to unwind after the day's events. She took a deep breath. There were a lot of changes that she hadn't considered, but felt that it would all turn out well.

Jim wasted no time the next day in getting his aunt's permission legally documented and recorded in the County Recorder's office. Next he added the information into the Certificate of Legal Access to the Resurvey listing the grantor and the recording data. The Ownership Certificate had been left blank till now. Jim made it out in both of their names, as an unmarried man and woman, since they were not married yet. After a final review Jim made the required number of copies and delivered them to the County Surveyor's office for filing. In about two weeks hopefully he should hear back if it was approved or not.

It was hard for Sarah to sleep that night, lapsing in and out of dreams about walking down the aisle and finding the missing ship filled with all kinds of treasure. She imagined herself sitting amidst open chests full of sparkling gold coins and glistening jewelry spilling out of them.

18

TRAPPED

Sarah went to work tired, but happy. She felt an inner glow within herself that was more than sustaining.

More and more valuables were coming out of the HMS Bristol day by day. Estimated value now exceeded several million dollars. Work would soon begin on the final ship, the HMS Andover, which was to commence in about eight to ten days.

There was much to think about concerning their marriage looming in the immediate future. Where would they live? Jim's place could work on a temporary basis, but not indefinitely. Where would they hold the ceremony? How many guests could they reasonably invite? There were so many decisions to be made; but Sarah felt that they were both reasonable and down-to-earth, and their likes and dislikes were very much compatible.

Also looming in her thoughts was the need to bring to justice the so-called pirates who had caused so much trouble, especially for her family. She was still quite angry about the abduction of her sister and all that they had put her through. The two men who were caught on the Griggsmore property were providing no clues to the identity or the whereabouts of the rest of the gang. One was apparently an American out of Baltimore and the other was a Brit. Did that indicate that someone outside of the area was orchestrating all the subterfuge? Probably so, she thought to herself. It was clever on Jim's part to set up a trap for the bad guys, and a bit risky as well. Nevertheless, after the trap had been sprung they still hadn't caught the ringleaders or put a stop to their activities.

What about the crumpled business card she found at the Tavern? She hadn't thought about that in quite some time. Was there a clue on the card? Sarah was determined to take another look.

There also was the lingering question as to who tipped off the crooks as to the discovery that had been made at the Lighthouse. It didn't make much sense that Mr. Kenton, Mr. Santee, or Mrs. Greer had anything to do with it. However, Owen did strongly object to being left out of the loop when Jim set up the sting operation. But on the other hand, after the pirates had vandalized the stone cabin it seemed that he knew nothing of its location. And it made no sense for Rick and Jennifer to be involved since they were supposedly dedicated to the preservation of history and historical artifacts.

What about Mr. Dubois who worked for the Preserve? Definitely a possibility she thought. But he had keys to the doors—why break the locks?

But what about the pilot and the deck hand who may have been wandering around the site while they were inside the Lighthouse? It came to her, that at the time, when she had seen shadow movement by one of the utility buildings, that the door of the Lighthouse had been left wide open. The Fresnel lens was sitting on a table just inside the doorway. Was it possible that one of them was lurking around and spying on their activities? Yes, absolutely, Sarah thought to herself.

Perhaps she should do some detective work and find out about those two guys who worked for the tour company. On the other hand, Jim would not want her to put herself in danger of any kind. But it was definitely tempting.

Sarah noticed that two members of the archeological team were busy marking out the location of the main excavation pit to access the fourth and final ship, the HMS Andover. The digging crew who would do the actual excavation and their equipment would not arrive for a number of days. Also marked out was where the spoils would be placed and the corners to where the fence was going to be extended.

Sarah made her rounds checking to see if all the protective barriers were in place and that there were no environmental issues.

Inside the security fence she noticed a lot of activity around the layout tables set up inside a long tent. There were stacks of coins, some silver, and some gold.

"Wow, what a sight to behold. Truly a fortune from a sunken treasure ship," commented Sarah. "Reminds me of the Atocha, which was found not that far down the coast," she added.

"Yes," replied a young woman who was one of the assistants, "but what makes this so much better is that we didn't have to dive to the bottom of the ocean to retrieve it or put it through an electrolysis process to remove all the encrustations."

"That's certainly true," realized Sarah.

The first stack was King George III silver schillings were mostly with the date of 1763. The next grouping was King George III gold guineas ranging in date from 1763 – 1767, and 1761. The dates on the coins all preceded the time of the wreck, which all made perfect sense.

"The gold coins are all 91.6 % pure gold. It was a standard that the British Government used for many years," informed the woman whose name was Clara Wright. Sarah noted her name on the photo ID that was on a lanyard that hung around her neck.

"I imagine these coins will be worth more than their weight in gold," assumed Sarah.

"Yes, they'll all be appraised for condition and no doubt their historical value will push their worth into the millions," believed Clara.

"Clara, are you by any chance related to the Wright Brothers, who made the first flight up in Kitty Hawk?" wondered Sarah.

171

"No, not directly," she answered. But they are a distant relative. Our branch of the family through my father's side was all centered in Columbus, quite some distance from Dayton, Ohio where they were from."

"Okay, I was just curious," replied Sarah shrugging her shoulders.

"I get that a lot," she smiled. "We'll have all this packaged up soon so you can sign off on these before they get shipped off," informed Clara.

Even though Jim's parents didn't have a lot of time to get to know their daughter-in-law better, they felt Sarah was a delightful match for their son. They bombarded Jim with all kinds of questions about their plans for and after the wedding. Frankly, he had to admit that they had not had a chance to talk about any of the details. Everyone was racing ahead trying to plan a wedding shower, and decorations for the reception, when he hadn't even purchased a proper engagement ring for his bride to be.

Jim had a busy day planned for working in the field, but managed to call Sarah at noon time to arrange to meet her after work to pick out their rings. Sarah readily agreed to meet him downtown at Mueller's Jewelry. Mueller's was a modest local shop catering to the needs of the locals.

Sarah found out that no other activity was planned for the Bristol site that day. That was good news, for she had the thought to do a little snooping. Remembering the business card she found at the Tavern, Sarah pulled it out to think about that potential clue. Did this have a connection with the so-called pirates? Maybe, she thought to herself. I could go in and look around, listen and observe. I'll put on a baseball cap or something to change my appearance and go incognito so to speak.

What was it that was scribbled in pencil on the backside of the card, numbers and a street name? The first figure could be a nine. The first part of what could be a name was —Blue. Blue what? The rest was faint and not distinguishable.

Driving into town, Sarah parked down the street from the pawn shop and readied herself. She found a hat on the backseat that read "Pelican Bay." Sarah thought that would give her a touristy look. Getting out she locked the car and proceeded down the sidewalk. Feeling a little nervous she reminded herself that there would probably be nothing to come out of this anyway.

A bell jingled as Sarah opened the heavy glass and wood door covered by metal bars. No one payed any attention as she came in. A shaggy-haired man behind the counter in the back was helping a middle-aged couple. They seemed to be dickering over some item. The room was basically a forty foot square and poorly lit. Framed sports memorabilia, art, old movie posters, and a couple of guitars lined the wall. Numerous items were displayed on tables scattered around the room. The more valuable items such as coins and jewelry were in glass counters lined along the back.

"Be right with you," finally called out the man behind the counter.

Sarah waved in recognition as she continued looking around. She gradually worked her way to the back counter at the opposite end from where the others were doing business. Individually packaged coins were displayed in the case. Many of them dated back to the Revolutionary War and even before. Confederate money was also displayed and government bonds paying two percent interest payable to the holder of the note. But since the South did not win, they were worthless, and now were just souvenirs. A large sign up on the wall advertised that they also purchased gold and silver.

Catching her attention were male voices coming out of a doorway that led into a backroom. Working her way over toward the doorway it almost sounded like they were arguing. Whatever it was about they sounded very unhappy. Walking past the doorway, Sarah thought she spotted someone moving around in the back. A second glance caught a closer look at the individual. Immediately, it struck her that she had seen this person before. Was he the one that peered at her through the window that night?

173

Perhaps it was. Sarah pulled down the bill of her hat to partially conceal her face.

In doing so, she looked down on the top of the glass case in front of her. Three business cards were taped on the underside of the glass. One of them was an antiques and fire arms store in Richmond, Virginia, named Richmond Hill. That name had a historical significance, because originally, Richmond Hill was in London, England, overlooking the Thames River. It was an interesting side note if nothing else.

"Young lady, how can I help you?" asked the salesman on the approach. He smiled at her.

"No, I don't see anything that catches my eye today," replied Sarah.

"Oh, there must be something of interest in here you would like," he grinned.

"There are some things of interest, but nothing I would like to purchase. Thank you though," she rebuffed.

"Perhaps another time," he encouraged.

"Yes, perhaps," remarked Sarah as she turned and walked out.

Once outside she speedily made her way back to the car. Opening the door she jumped inside and slammed the door shut. After locking the door Sarah took a deep breath. Taking a few moments to compose herself, she realized what she needed to do was to drive around and observe the back of the pawn shop.

In doing so Sarah drove around the corner and positioned herself along the side street to where she could see down an alleyway to the back of the store. Sarah looked at her watch and thumped her fingers on the armrest. It wouldn't be too long before she had to meet Jim.

Sarah did not have to wait long before the man she had spotted in the store came out. He clearly was dark haired and had a facial beard. She estimated his age between twenty-five and thirty. He went directly to a beat-up pickup parked in the alleyway and started it up. Sarah watched as he drove up the alley away from her.

Though inadvisable, Sarah thought she would try following at a safe distance. Starting her car up she followed up through the alley and out onto the busy street, turning right. Sarah stayed quite a distance back so as not to be so obvious. The man was definitely heading out of town. She followed him for about two miles at what she thought was a safe distance. He forked left onto a different road then right onto another. Coming around a corner the beat-up pickup was suddenly just ahead of her. Woe! What's happening she wondered? Sarah quickly slowed keeping her distance. Was he checking her out?

Suddenly the pickup truck accelerated away from her and disappeared around a curve in the road. She didn't know if she should proceed any further, but kept going slowly. Sarah went around the curve and did not see him anywhere. After a few moments she noticed movement in her rear view mirror. Her heart sank when she realized that he was now behind her and accelerating.

Sarah stomped on it, but quickly realized she didn't have the speed to outrun him. Coming around another turn in the road the pickup quickly gained on her and hit the car's rear bumper causing her a temporarily loss of control. Her heart pounded in her chest. Jim and her marriage flashed through her thoughts. Sarah spotted a dirt driveway veering off to the right. He was accelerating again, but before he could ram her again she hit her brakes and steered into the driveway. A split second later the pursuing vehicle hit the back right corner of the car spinning her around off the pavement and into the partially overgrown driveway.

Almost at the very same instant a County Sheriff's car appeared coming from the opposite direction and observed the last part of the altercation. The pickup truck skidded to a stop sideways in the right-hand lane, but quickly sped off down the road.

Sarah was knocked around a bit and felt somewhat dizzy. She sat there trying to get her composure back. The officer sprang out of his car and ran over to see if Sarah was okay. He tapped on her side window to get her attention. Realizing that it was an officer she quickly rolled down the window and replied she was fine.

"Go after him, he tried to run me off the road," demanded Sarah.

"Okay, I just wanted to check on your condition first," he replied. "Sit tight; I'll need a statement from you on this incident." With that he ran back to his vehicle, turned on his sirens, and swung around to pursue the pickup.

"My goodness, what is mom and Jim going to say about this," she realized thinking about the fallout from this incident.

Getting out of her vehicle see looked to see what damage her car had sustained. On the right rear corner was a large dent in the bumper and a ugly crease in the adjoining fender.

"Great!" Sarah declared. "This just adds to the score that I need to settle with these scoundrels.

Looking at her watch Sarah realized she needed to call Jim and let him know she would be a few minutes late. But before Sarah could do so the patrol car returned without any success in apprehending the assailant. The officer went ahead and made out a report on the incident, classifying it as a hit-and-run.

"Say, you're the young lady that works for Jim Hollingsworth," he suddenly realized. "And you're involved in all the ruckus over the lost treasure ships."

"Ruckus is right," confirmed Sarah. "Matter of fact I believe I was following one of the crooks, and it appears that I was proven right.

"I'll need a description of the person and the vehicle," he replied.

"Let me share something with you that might shed even more light on this whole thing," she announced.

Reaching into her car she grabbed her purse and retrieved the tattered business card that she had found at the Tavern.

"I found this card at the Track of the Lion Tavern, after it was vandalized a while back," explained Sarah.

"Southern Treasures," read off the officer.

"I wondered if there was a connection, so I hung out there for a while today to observe if there was anything of a suspicious nature going on," she continued. "That's when I spotted a man at the back of the business that seemed familiar, so I followed him. And boom! Here I am."

"Hmm," considered the officer. "You shouldn't have done that."

"I know," she whined. "Oh," Sarah remembered, "on the back is an address or something written in pencil. I haven't been able to read though."

"I'll see if the boys in the lab can read it," he replied poking it in his shirt pocket.

After gathering the remainder of the information he needed for the report, the officer left and Sarah headed back to town. She glanced at her watch seeing that she was about ten minutes late for her appointment. Coming down Main Street and rounding a corner Sarah spotted him standing outside the jewelry store. The thought occurred to her that maybe she shouldn't say anything to him about this latest incident. But on the other hand she didn't want to start the practice of hiding things from her soon to be husband. Finding a parking space down a short ways, Sarah bounded across the street to meet him.

"Sorry I'm late," apologized Sarah a little out of breath.

"I thought for a moment you had changed your mind," stated Jim giving her a quick hug and kiss.

"No, not at all," she replied. "Jim, don't get mad at me, but I went down to the Southern Treasures Pawn Shop and was doing some snooping around. And low and behold I spotted this guy that looked familiar."

"Sar-ah!" he scolded. "You know better not to put yourself in danger like that."

"I know and I'm sorry, it was not the right thing to do. Because when I followed him he tried to run me off the road. He hit my rear bumper and spun me around just as a Sheriff's patrol car came around the corner. But I'm fine and the crook got away."

177

"My goodness, Sarah," reacted Jim hugging her again.

"And, yes, if I'm going to be your wife, I can't be doing things like that," she stated.

Jim just shook his head and took a deep breath. "Yes," he reaffirmed. "Shall we see about some rings? That is if you're still up to it?

"Oh, yes," responded Sarah. "This is a very special occasion."

Stepping into the jewelry store, they asked for help and were directed to a particular glass display case. Sarah asked Jim his opinion on certain ones. Jim smiled at seeing how she went through the decision making process, selecting what was more practical and not gaudy.

"I like this one," she finally replied holding her hand out looking at it in the varying light. "See how it sparkles."

"Just like your eyes," observed Jim.

Sarah smiled at him and gave him an emotional hug. "Thank you," she whispered in his ear.

A couple of days later, Jim sat down to review the books on the business to see if they were keeping their heads above water financially. After nearly three hours of review it appeared they were just getting by. One thing in their favor was the fact that a couple of completed jobs had not yet been billed out. Any revenue from the shipwrecks probably would not be realized for a year or two. So anything from that source would not be of any immediate help.

On a personal note, if the Resurvey came through, the County would be asking for property tax in short order. There also was going to be wedding expenses that would be coming up. Jim laughed to himself thinking how he could ask Sarah if she would be agreeable to a barn wedding. No, I think we can do much better than that, he concluded.

Other changes were soon to come. Sarah would soon be finishing her job at the Griggsmore property and returning to join him in the field crew. That would be a new dynamic being a married couple working together, but he looked forward to that.

The big day finally came when Jim received the word that the Resurvey was ready to record except for one minor correction that had to be made. Later in the day he went by the County Surveyor's Office to make the correction and found out that a similar re-survey for the same property had also been submitted. But since the Hollingsworth Survey was now approved to be recorded, the other resurvey would have their submission and fees returned to them. Jim was surprised that the other survey company was able to make up so much ground and almost beat him to the punch.

Jim was happy to give everyone the good news that the berry patch property was to be recorded both in his and Sarah's name sometime during the following morning. A parcel number would soon be assigned to the property and ultimately a tax bill would be forth coming. That part he wasn't so happy about.

There was excitement from both families wanting to come out and see the property including his father who was feeling much better. And so it was after a couple of days they all planned to meet out there to have a look around.

On that particular day everyone first received a guided tour of the uniquely shaped property including the location of the future driveway that would be along the granted access easement. That strip would soon have to be cleared of trees and vegetation.

Sarah related it was the wild blueberry patch that first attracted her to the property. And how through the accidental discovery of a granite stepping stone that led her and Sadie to search back into the trees to see where it was leading to.

"That's when Sarah fell into the hole," added Sadie.

"Yes, that was quite embarrassing, I must say," commented Sarah. "But, it was that, which brought Jim to my rescue," she smiled.

"Sarah came to me, wanting to find out who owned this property," recalled Jim. "And so it began. I soon realized there was something unusual going on with this land. We formed a partnership to explore this further. Sarah even agreed to come

179

out on the survey crew to help out. From there, boom, boom, bang and here we are."

"And think of it," spoke up Sarah's mom, "there was a buried treasure ship on the property and an old family letter that held clues to its location."

"That's our next stop," announced Jim, "the stone cabin and the remains of the HMS Blackpool. Watch your step. There's still a lot of tripping hazards."

"Oh," realized Sadie, "I forgot my phone back at the car."

"Better hurry and catch up with us," replied her mother.

"Be right back," she answered heading back across the meadow.

Meanwhile, everyone else slowly made their way through the trees to finally arrive in front of the stone cabin. Jim opened up the heavy door.

"As you can see, this stone structure has been well hidden in this jungle of trees and vines for some two hundred years," stated Sarah.

"So, is this where the stepping stones led you to?" asked Jim's dad.

"Yes, basically, it got me close enough to where I was able to get a visual on it," she answered.

"Were you able to get right in?" he further asked.

"No, far from it," replied Sarah. "Jim had to bring his chainsaw and cut this big beam up and pull this heavy ship's chain off of it," she pointed.

"This was some fortified building," commented Mrs. Bentley.

Jim's dad stepped into the building, turned his light on and began looking around. Sarah's mother was a bit concerned that Sadie had not yet returned.

"She has already seen the cabin," recalled Sarah. "Maybe she may not be so interested in seeing it again."

"Yeah, she'll be along," seconded her mom.

Jim explained how the table when it was raised up, opened up the floor giving access to the stairway leading down into the ship. They could see how the floor was all tore up and the table was trashed, which the so-called pirates caused when they broke in.

"Be careful when going down the stairs," he warned. "They are not in the best of condition."

Slowly they worked their way down the steps to arrive in the hallway of the ship.

"You are now inside the eighteenth century British ship, the HMS Blackpool," declared Sarah.

Meanwhile, while they were showing them around in the interior of the ship, Sadie had made her way back to where the cars were parked. She had a good idea where she had left her phone. Bent over and going through a bag setting on the backseat of their car she quickly located it.

Suddenly she heard a noise coming from down the dirt road coming toward her. Sadie spotted a couple of pickup trucks speeding in her direction. They didn't look friendly. She closed the backdoor and heard it go click as she crouched down behind the car. The vehicles stopped a short distance away. There was angry talking at first. Sadie was able to make out a few words from the muddle of voices. Something about, "They better tell us what we want, or else …"

A pang ran through her, as she realized it was the pirates again. She crouched down even further with her back up against the rear tire. Her hands trembled. What was she going to do?

Soon their voices became silent as they advanced across the meadow. Sadie rose up and peeked through the rear side windows. They were all gone. She now knew exactly what had to be done. Her hands were still shaking as she dialed 911.

Jim's dad was fascinated by the ship's construction as they worked their way down the hall toward the aft of the ship. Sarah's mom thought it was all a bit creepy working their way around in the dark.

Loud noises emanated from above causing everyone to look back down the hallway.

"Sadie, is that you?" questioned Sarah.

"Hollingsworth! Are you down there?" came an angry voice down the stairwell. There was dead silence for a moment with everyone wondering who it was and what they wanted. There was a hint of a English accent in the man's words.

"Yes," spoke up Jim. "Who's asking?" he inquired. "You realize you're trespassing on private property, don't you?"

"Never mind," responded the grumpy voice. "I need to know where the fourth ship is located. I have a couple sticks of dynamite here to seal your fate if you don't answer. I know your family is probably down there with you, besides your girlfriend. If you really care about them you won't hesitate to give me the information."

Jim could tell everyone was quite frightened by this sudden change of circumstances. Sarah's mom had the appearance of going into a panic attack.

"Who is to say you won't toss the dynamite down here even if I did give you the information?" questioned Jim.

"You'll have to take that chance," he responded. "You have little choice. Besides, the contents of that ship and the others do not belong to you or to this renegade nation."

"I'm coming up there to talk some sense into you," informed Jim who also getting quite agitated.

"No you're not. You wouldn't get half way up the stairs before you got plugged," threatened the stranger.

Sarah grabbed Jim around his midsection tightly. "No, you're going up there," she demanded. "What are you going to do? We don't know for sure where the last ship is located," she whispered.

"I have my lighter going, you better cough up the info, or it's going to be curtains," he again called out. A long silent pause ensued. "This would be a fitting tomb for you, considering all the trouble you've given us. This will sink your ship and you with it. Very well, I'm lighting the fuse."

Sarah and her mother gasped. Jim considered fabricating something concerning the possibility that it was next to the other ship to give them more time, but before he could reply, they could hear loud talking and warning shouts. Something was definitely going amiss.

"Too bad for you folks," again spoke up the same voice.

Suddenly, they heard a clunk on the stairway and something tumbling down toward them which landed right at Jim's feet. A burning fuse was readily visible along with what must have been a couple of sticks of dynamite. Sarah and her mom screamed. Jim's dad let out a loud cry. Jim quickly stomped on the fuse and separated it from the explosives.

"Wow! That was close," he stated realizing that the immediate danger was over.

Sarah and her mom both were trying to catch their breath and regain their composure.

"I thought for a moment that we were all goners," responded Mrs. Bentley.

"What about Sadie?" realized Sarah. "She's up there somewhere."

"They're probably long gone," believed Jim. "Let's get up there and find Sadie as quick as we can."

Everyone agreed and hurried up the stairway. On the way, Jim snatched up the two sticks of dynamite. Sarah was concerned that they could still go off, but he replied it was now safe.

No one was around as they emerged back up into the cabin and out into the daylight. At that moment Jim threw down the two sticks of dynamite and began laughing.

"What is so funny?" questioned Sarah.

"They tricked us," he answered. "It's not dynamite. They were just flares."

Jim's dad looked down at them. "You're right son, they're just road flares," he confirmed.

"We have to find Sadie," reminded Sarah.

"Yes," agreed Jim.

At that he took off like a bolt through the trees leaving the others behind. Jim could hear talking and what sounded like the opening and closing of vehicle doors. Coming out into the clearing he could make out police vehicles with their lights flashing. A couple of officers were coming toward him with Sadie leading them.

"Sadie!" came the yell from behind him.

Sarah and her mom raced up and hugged Sadie, asking if she was alright. Sadie said she was. Matter of fact, she disclosed that she called 911 and hid behind their car when the bad guys suddenly arrived.

"They ran off through the brush scattering like wild turkeys when we arrived," informed one of the officers.

"That's what they were so upset about," now realized Jim. "It wasn't the dynamite, which it wasn't, but it was the arrival of the Sheriff's Department."

"In all the confusion, they somehow were able to make off with one of their vehicles," added the other officer.

"They keep slipping through our fingers," protested Sarah.

"Miss Bentley, I'm Deputy Harris and if you remember I was the one you gave the business card to, after that run in you had with that pickup just outside of town," reintroduced the first officer.

"Oh, yes, I do remember you now," she answered.

"Sarah? What incident did you have outside of town?" questioned her mother.

"I'll tell you about it later," Sarah replied.

"It's because of that card we have a lead," he continued. "It was forwarded to the State Lab in Charleston for analysis. They were able to read what was written on the back of the card and apparently it is an address.

"Where?" Sarah demanded.

"Sar-ah!" spoke up Jim.

"No, but I sure would like to know," she replied.

19

"TRUST NO ONE"

Two days later they were informed that the Sheriff's Dept. did in fact make a raid on a property located on Bluefordtown Rd. in Nesmith about ten miles northwest of Georgetown. They were successful in apprehending five crude looking characters holding out in an old shop building hidden back in the woods. Incriminating evidence was found in abundance which included the items stolen from the HMS Blackpool, and many illegal firearms. But nothing turned up that indicated who they were working for. None of them would co-operate; and asked for an attorney.

A sixth person was also taken into custody who happened along later. On seeing the police presence he tried to make a run for it, but he was apprehended down the road a short distance. There was no direct proof that this person was involved with this gang. However, he did have a police record that included incidents that happened in a number of European countries.

Sarah was asked to come in and see if she recognized any of the criminals. At the Sheriff's office there was a special room with a large television monitor. They placed her in a chair to watch the screen as they paraded the fugitives one by one in front of the camera in the next room. The second person they brought in she recognized as the deck hand on the Dixie Express. Yes, that made sense she told herself. The fourth person was also quite recognizable. It was the young man with black hair and a short beard. The one who was prowling around their house and then also tried running her off the road. It made her a bit nervous seeing him again. The next person she did not recognize at all.

The final person that came on the screen Sarah also did not recognize, but he was definitely very tall. But wait! Wasn't the person, Sadie and her had seen from a distance across the meadow at the blueberry patch quite tall? And wasn't he very allergic to the ragweed?

"This isn't like a smoking gun or anything, but I may have a way to see if this is the person I saw snooping around the property where the stone cabin is located," informed Sarah.

"How so?" she was asked.

"Well, the person we saw was highly allergic to ragweed. Do you have any ragweed around the station," wondered Sarah.

"We do," laughed the deputy. "I'll be right back."

Soon the deputy reappeared on the monitor screen in the other room with a handful of weeds. Waving them around the man began violently sneezing. After which he was led away.

"Definitely circumstantial evidence, but it's an indicator that we should have a closer look at this person," remarked the officer on his return. "He has a record that spans the ocean, all the way over to England."

"That reminds me, when I was in Southern Treasures snooping around, I saw a business card that was for an antiques and firearms store in Richmond Virginia that was named Richmond Hill. What struck me was that Richmond Hill was originally in London overlooking the Thames River. The thought occurred to me that there may be a British connection in all this."

"Hmm, that's interesting you would pick up on that," commented the deputy.

"History was one of my favorite courses while I was in college," replied Sarah.

"Okay, thank you for your help today. If we need your further assistance we will be in contact," he finalized escorting her out.

Four days later, they learned that efforts to find the fourth ship on the Griggsmore property had failed. This was quite unexpected. The wood structure that was found during the pothole excavation proved to be some kind of temporary deck positioned beside the HMS Bristol. The location of the last ship was apparently still unknown. Sarah realized her work out at that property would probably soon be coming to an end.

Next day another shoe dropped. Jim was informed through the State Historical Commission that a decision had been handed down by the Justice Department and the State Department rejecting a British claim on the contents of the four British ships stating that maritime law did not hold any precedent in this case and was in itself a precursor to war against the colonists seeking independence from Britain.

The significance of this reality didn't hit home at first, because up to that time there was little they could claim from any of the ship wreck discoveries.

That evening Sarah went home and looked at all the things in her bedroom and closet contemplating what things she would pack up and initially move over after the wedding. That's right, they hadn't set a date yet, she reminded herself. Maybe Jim needs a little prompting.

Sarah caught sight of the envelope that contained the old letter lying on her desk. Where is the missing ship she wondered? Grabbing it up she sat down and reread the old letter reviewing the clues that it gave. The strange thing was, they had followed the clues and found three of the ships, but not the fourth. And so far there was no indication of where the two keys were to be used. It had to be on the very last ship or in another location.

It was during the night while sleeping she had dreams about the missing ship and the old letter.

"Jim! Jim!" Sarah called out suddenly awakening. "Oh, what time is it?"

"Sarah, are you okay?" inquired her sister getting out of bed.

"I need Jim," she stated in a matter of fact tone.

"Can't you wait till the wedding day?" asked Sadie half asleep.

"What? No, I mean yes!" replied Sarah. "I think I know where the fourth ship is."

"Really? You were thinking about that in the middle of the night?" questioned her sister.

"I had a dream. I saw it perfectly," she answered. "You have to go with us tomorrow."

"Oh, I guess," she yawned, "as long as there are no more pirates."

"No, I don't believe so," replied her older sister.

Next morning Sarah was up early and gave Jim a call at his house and insisted they had to go out to the berry patch as soon as they could go.

"I think I know where the missing ship is located," she told him. "And bring your key."

"And where do we find this allusive ship?" he wanted to know.

"I'll show you when we get there," answered Sarah. "The answer was right in front of us the whole time."

After an hour Jim came by and picked up Sarah and Sadie, and headed over to the berry patch. It was on the way that Sarah remembered they needed to talk about another important topic.

"Oh, on another very important subject," spoke up Sarah. "We need to set a wedding date."

Jim looked at his watch. "How about five o'clock?" Sadie laughed.

"What? No, seriously," she asked.

"It should be before the weather starts turning, probably no more than a month," he proposed. "That should give everyone time to make preparations I would think."

"Sounds good," replied Sarah. "I'll look on the calendar and see what Saturday would fit that."

Once at the site, Jim questioned Sarah what things they would need to find the missing ship.

"We'll be going down into the ship, so we'll need lights, a pry bar, and probably a hammer," she stated. "After that I don't know."

Packing the tools with them they soon arrived at the stone cabin. Once inside Sarah flashed her light on the back wall above where the table used to sit.

"Take note of what that sign says: Trust No One," she pointed out.

"Okay, now what?" asked Jim.

"Follow me down into the ship," directed Sarah.

"After you, Sadie," motioned Jim.

"Sarah, this better not be a wild goose chase," warned Sadie.

"I'm very hopeful that will not be the case," she replied.

Stepping down into the dark domain they finally reached the main hallway that ran the ship. Sarah waited till everyone was down off of the stairway.

"Our destination is the Great Room which is on the next level," informed Sarah.

She led them down through the opening in the floor to the hallway below. From there it was another fifty feet toward the aft of the ship. Once inside the room Sarah flashed the light around looking at the various features that the room presented.

"Please notice the second sign that says: Trust no one," pointed out Sarah. "Where was the first sign located?" she asked rhetorically.

"On the wall above the table as I recall," spoke up Sadie.

"Yes, just above where the entrance to the ship was located," pointed out her sister.

"So, you're saying there is another entrance, here, under the second sign," deducted Jim.

"Correct! I believe that phrase is more than just a warning, it's really a clue," she believed. "It was written at the bottom of the old letter along with the other clues."

"It also was written in the ship's log book as well," remembered Jim.

"That's true, I'd forgotten that," realized Sarah. "Anyway, I believe that the entrance to the HMS Andover is right behind here," she indicated tapping the cabinets along the left wall.

"What you're saying does make sense," pondered Jim.

Sadie opened one of the cabinet doors and found that the shelves were all empty. She knocked on the back wall but couldn't tell if it was hollow behind.

Everyone began a thorough search through the various parts of the sprawling cabinetry. Some sections had doors and others did not. After much effort, nothing yielded a clue. Everything seemed to be solid and unmovable.

"The rough-sawn boards are thick enough to prevent us from hearing any hollow spots," contemplated Jim.

"Hmm," considered Sarah. Getting down on her hands and knees she ran her light along the baseboard of the cabinet. "Well, that's interesting," she commented.

"What do you see?" asked Sadie.

"From this point over to the left, the cabinet does not touch the floor," she pointed out using the flashlight. "There is about an inch and a half gap."

"Really?" considered Jim.

With that in mind he went to the left of that section and shined his light along the wall, but found no gaps or openings. Stepping back he searched along the top of the woodwork.

"Well, I'll be" spotlighted Jim.

"Looks like a series of those finials that were used on the table upstairs," recognized Sarah.

"If that is true they could be a trigger of sorts just as they were on the table," he added.

"You'll need something to stand on," realized Sarah.

"There were some loose boards just down the hallway a short ways," recalled Sadie.

"Good suggestion," complemented Jim.

It wasn't long before they had located the boards and stacked them up in front of the cabinet. They proved to be a bit wobbly.

"If you guys help steady me I think I can reach up there," he requested.

"Sadie, you get that side I'll hold on this side," directed her sister.

Jim reached up and examined the vertical protruding knobs. "Their similar to the others, but not exact," he reported.

"Try pulling or pushing on them," suggested Sarah.

"Okay-y," he replied. "I'll start with the first one on the right. After a brief struggle it would not budge. "No go. Let me try the next one." It was the same on the second one. Going on to the third finial Jim pulled on it, but it snapped. "Well, that one is not going to co-operate."

"Well, it's the ninth inning with two out and the final batter coming to the plate," stated Sarah.

"Ha! I didn't know you liked baseball," he replied.

"Slow pitch softball," interjected Sadie.

"Yeah, that's true," she confirmed.

Jim pulled on the next finial and rod, but it too refused to budge. "That's not good," he commented.

"No! That can't be right!" protested Sarah.

"I didn't have a strong grip. Let me try that again, he declared. He pulled again making a gr-r-r sound.

"Hear that?" pointed out Sadie. "It's the sound of your future husband getting mad at you," she laughed.

"Sadie! Be nice," scolded Sarah.

Suddenly there was a loud pop and everyone froze wondering what had happened.

"Hope I didn't break something down inside," stated Jim as he pulled a lengthy rod and finial all the way out.

Stepping down off the stack of boards he grabbed the whole cabinet about five feet from the end and gave it a violent jerk. All the cabinets along the wall rumbled and a whole section swung open revealing another doorway behind. Sarah was stunned.

"Sarah, looks like you were right," declared her sister. "But now what are we in for?"

20

THE MISSING SHIP

"Well Sarah, the logbook did say for 'British eyes only,' and so far you've had the many clues pegged correctly," praised Jim.

"I felt I had to figure this out. The letter has been in our family for generations without any resolution. It just had to get solved. Besides it wasn't just me. Jim, your family was apparently involved in this also and with your knowledge of land surveying, that's what really launched this discovery forward. And Sadie, you really have been a help all along the way," replied Sarah.

Jim noticed writing above the doorway. "What does that say?" he questioned lifting up his light.

"It says: Beware, Danger," made out his fiancée, reading it slowly.

"Danger from what?" questioned Sadie.

"Probably from something on the other side of the door," he reasoned.

"Oh-h, look at this," discovered Sarah, "keyholes, on the right side of the door, one above the other one."

"There, finally!" excitely responded Jim. "So, this is where the keys come into play."

"I was beginning to wonder about that myself," she commented.

"Dual locks," considered Sadie. "One has an H and the other a B."

"So it does," observed Sarah. "The H and the B again is showing us the way. But do we dare open it?"

"I believe we're safe on this side of the door," stated Jim looking at the ceiling and floor in front of the door area.

Sarah found her key and inserted it into the keyhole on the bottom. Turning the key proved to be difficult, but it finally rotated in the lock. Jim dug his key out and placed it in the other lock mechanism. After he turned his key, Jim gave the door a push and it opened slightly. Almost instantly they heard a dreadful noise like something heavy sliding down behind the wall and the sound of chains rattling.

"What just happened?" wondered Sadie.

"There is only one way to find out," answered Jim pushing the door all the way open.

"Careful," cautioned Sarah.

Jim stuck his head through the opening while holding on to the door frame and began examining what was in the darkness beyond.

"Huh, there's a bridge out here," he informed.

"Bridge? How can that be?" questioned Sarah.

Jim reached up and jerked on something and instantly they could hear a swaying noise with the sound of wood clacking.

"What is that?" asked both sisters.

"It's a suspended walkway of sorts made up of barrel staves," he answered. Shining his light down between the slats Jim made a new discovery. "There's also a deep hole underneath here that must go all the way down to the original river bed that the ship is resting on."

"Jim, I'm dying to know," spoke up Sarah. "Is there another ship over there?"

"Ah-h, there is an open doorway on the other side, and it appears that I am seeing a hull of another ship," he believed. "Yes! We have found the fourth ship."

"E-ha! Mystery solved!" she exclaimed.

"What about the walkway, is it safe to cross?" wondered Sadie who was trying to sneak a peek.

193

"That is a good question," he considered. "I'll try placing part of my body weight on the first section."

They could hear the walkway groan and sway a bit, but it held tight. Jim placed all his weight on it and again it felt solid.

"Chains are the main support system and it appears they are still maintaining their integrity," observed Jim.

He backed up and made a short jump on the first section to test it further. The swaying walkway jerked and rattled with a great noise. Jim made a couple steps out onto the bridge.

"Oh, wow," he noticed training his light on the ceiling. "Large timbers are holding the ground above in place. But as I follow the path of the support chains back to their anchor point it appears they were designed to release and send intruders into the pit."

"Grab my hand. I want you back where it's safe," beckoned Sarah.

"It's okay; we used the keys which disarmed the booby trap it so appears," believed Jim.

"Yes, but it could still fail," she protested.

Ignoring that comment, Jim advanced further across the bridge which lurched and swayed as he went. He could clearly make out the weathered boards of a ship's hull as he neared the doorway. Shining his light into the dark void Jim could only make out walls and partitions.

"I'm across," he announced. "But stay put, I coming back over."

The walkway popped and creaked as he walked aggressively back toward them.

"I do believe it's safe," concluded Jim.

"Ah, if you don't mind I'm going to stay right here," determined Sadie.

"That's fine," he replied. "Sarah, if you want to wait here also, while I check it out?"

"Oh, no, I have to see what's over there, especially after all that we've went through on this," she responded.

"Okay, follow me," replied Jim.

As Sarah followed she had to stop and gather her balance as the suspended walkway swayed and lurched. This was quite nerve-racking to say the least. It seemed like forever to traverse the twenty foot span over to the other ship.

"Sadie, are you going to be alright by yourself for a few minutes?" asked Sarah.

"Yes, I'll be fine," she reassured her. "But nothing better happen to you guys because I'll be out a babysitting job later on."

Sarah laughed. "Sadie! You really surprise me sometimes. The things you say."

As they worked their way to the main corridor that ran the length of the ship it was noticed that everything appeared to have been cleared out. That proved to be true as they searched forward in the ship and then back in the opposite direction.

"This is odd," stated Sarah. "Almost like everything was cleared out and moved over to the Bristol, or to some other location."

"It almost gives you that impression, but maybe that's just what they want an unwanted intruder to think," replied Jim.

Unexpectedly, the hallway widened out and a wood wall confronted them stopping their progress. A single door located in the center was the only visible means of passage.

"Could this be it? Right through there?" hoped Sarah.

"Open it and find out," he suggested.

"I'm a little apprehensive," she confessed. "An axe could come flying out of the darkness."

"You have a vivid imagination," commented Jim.

He cracked open the door slightly and flashed his light around, but could not see anything. Sarah was pressed up against him, holding her light up high so she also could get a glimpse into the room. Finally, Jim pushed the door all the way open. Once inside their light beams crisscrossed searching out the extremities of the room. Sarah took a deep breath.

"Nothing here," concluded Jim.

Sarah was so disappointed that she couldn't speak at first. Both continued to scour the walls for clues, but nothing was found.

"This is so frustrating!" she finally exclaimed. "I'm going back out to the main room."

"We're at an apparent dead-end," reckoned Jim.

Both stepped back into the larger room glancing around for anything they had missed on the first run through.

"What's this in the floor over here?" noticed Sarah walking to her right. "There's a small square panel and it appears to have a lock mechanism centered in it. And oh! There is an H next to the key hole!"

"Really? How did we miss that?" he rhetorically asked.

"Probably because we were so busy looking at the walls that we neglected what was at our feet," figured Sarah.

"If there is one, there must be the other," reasoned Jim.

Turning, they directed their attention to the same general area on the opposite side of the room to locate the second lock mechanism. And there it was, designated by a B.

"The locks are so far apart this time," she considered.

"The reasoning has to be that it takes the cooperation of two parties, using the different keys to complete the unlocking procedure," contemplated Jim.

"Kinda like initiating the launch codes in a missile silo," laughed Sarah.

"Exactly," he replied. "Put your key in and I'll so the same, and let's see what happens."

"Hopefully, the floor won't open up and swallow us," she commented.

"Or daggers come down out of the ceiling," he added shining his light on the wooden ceiling above."

"I can't get my key to turn as hard as I try," announced Sarah.

"Hmm, mine won't turn either," seconded Jim.

"Perhaps Jim, as you alluded to earlier, it has to be done, together," she suggested.

"Okay, ready? Both at the same time, go," he stated.

There was a loud click as both keys with the combined effort successfully turned in their mechanisms. Suddenly, a loud ratcheting sound could be heard and then the whole floor they were standing on jerked and dropped six inches. Sarah was startled and gave off a short cry as she reached over to grab Jim to stabilize herself.

"Hang on, we're going down," yelled Jim wrapping his arm around her.

The floor continued to drop, not completely level, but descend it did. It hit bottom with a mild crash. Then there were walls right, left, and behind them in the bottom level of the ship. But directly in front of them, underneath the room they were just in was a partitioned-off chamber. Stacked chests and boxes were discernible on the left and groupings of unrecognizable slender vertical shafts on the right. Both of their lights were beginning to run down and it was harder to see anything in real detail.

"You okay in there?" called out Sadie.

"Yes, we're fine," Sarah yelled back.

"What is all this?" wondered Jim stepping up to take a closer look. "Oh!" he exclaimed.

"They are single-shot British military rifles," she recognized.

"There must be over five hundred in here," estimated Jim. "Enough for a small army," he considered. "And it almost appears they have never been used."

"I'm curious to know what's in these wood boxes and chests," stated Sarah turning her attention to the huge stack of containers on the left.

"There is row after row going back some thirty feet," observed Jim.

Opening a box next to her, she peered inside, but was unsure at first what the contents were.

"It must be ammunition, if I'm not mistaken," Sarah finally realized.

"There are hand guns in this box over here," he reported. "The British were indeed preparing to go to war over these colonies."

"Jim! Look at these chests back here!" she exclaimed. "They are so ornate, and look at the rings attached to the sides."

"Huh, that is different," he recognized.

"They have locks on them," observed Sarah.

"Try your key?" suggested Jim.

"I wonder," she replied. Retrieving the skeleton key from her pocket she tried it in the lock. "It fits, but as usual I can't turn it."

"That's why women have to have men around," stated Jim.

"To unlock things?" she questioned.

"Well, to open jars and such things," he explained.

"Oh," she laughed. "I think there are other good reasons besides that."

"I'm glad you think so," replied Jim.

Jim worked the key back and forth until it finally turned. Jerking on it, it snapped open. Removing the lock he raised the lid.

"Oh my!" exclaimed Sarah. "The treasure is still here! After all we've been through; it was under our very noses the whole time."

"Gold coins of some kind," he observed stirring them around and picking up one.

"Gold guineas," she recognized. "I saw stacks of them over at the other ship."

Must be at least two dozen of these chests," guessed Jim. "Definitely, a great fortune," he surmised.

"I wonder though, how much of this we will be able to keep?" considered Sarah taking a deep breath.

"Well, the State Historical Commission has already signed off on this site and the Federal Government has already debunked any foreign claims," he commented. "So, the chances are good."

"That would be nice," she replied. "We could then afford to build our home on this property."

"That would be a wonderful reality," agreed Jim. "But at this point in time you are an unmarried woman who owns fifty percent interest of the property, and now, all of this as well. You could stay single, sell your half of the land and take your half of the treasure with you."

"Jim, are you testing my love for you?" she questioned.

"I'm wondering, now that we have found the treasure, if it will make any difference in our relationship?" asked Jim.

"No, like I said before. You are my real treasure," she answered. "All of this may just go away, but I want to be with you forever."

"Thank you for that," he praised her, "and I feel the same."

Reaching for each other they hugged and kissed and shed a few tears.

"Hey! What's going on in there?" called out Sadie.

"We'll be right out," yelled back Sarah drying her tears.

Jim picked up three or four gold coins and closed the lid on the chest. It suddenly donned on them they were on a level below the main corridor. How were they going to get back up?

"There's our answer," finally discovered Sarah, "a stairway along the side. But, wait, it doesn't go all the way up," she realized.

"I see what they did," understood Jim. "There is a short section of steps that is hinged back onto the staircase. All we have to do is go up and flip it over, and walk on out."

"Wow, I'm impressed with all their handiwork," appreciatively commented Sarah.

Once up, they worked their way back down the dark hallway and out to where they entered the ship. Crossing the makeshift suspension bridge they quickly made it across to the other side.

"Doing okay?" asked Sarah.

"Yes, fine, except it's kind of creepy here in the darkness all alone," she answered. "But I was worried about, you guys. I could hear you talking, and there was that terrible rumbling noise, and then I heard Sarah shriek."

Sarah laughed. "Yes, I did."

"Well! Are you going to tell me?" she asked gesturing with her hands.

Jim reached in his pocket. "Sadie, hold out your hand, " he ordered.

Complying she held her hand out and he proceeded to drop into her hand two gold coins.

"You found, the treasure!" she realized.

"Sadie, you must keep this quiet for now," instructed her sister.

"Wow, what a wedding gift," pondered Sadie.

"True, but Sadie, the real treasure is finding someone you can spend the rest of your life with," shared Sarah.

"I'm very happy for you both," she smiled.

In the months that followed, Jim and Sarah did get married; and for a time made due living in Jim's small house while their plans were being finalized for their new home on the berry patch property.

Living together and working together seemed to cement their relationship evermore quickly. The office too had to go through an adjustment as well, now that Sarah was married to the boss and was gradually learning the various other aspects of running the business. She still enjoyed going out into the field working with Jim and Billy.

As for the treasure, it was pretty much still intact being stored in a high security vault. No government agency was able to lay a claim on it. However, whenever they had to sell an allotment of the coins, IRS was right there to get their portion.

Sadie was elated to know that her educational fund for the future was secure. Sarah's mother was very happy for the newlyweds and appreciated Jim's help whenever there was a household emergency to repair. Jim's father was improving in health and they were able to catch up with all their medical bills.

As for those troublesome pirates, all of them were sent 'up river' to spend jail time for their various crimes which included kidnapping. Additionally, Sarah's tip concerning Richmond Hill proved fruitful. Further investigation led law enforcement to the owner of the business in London, England, who was a wealthy financier who dabbled in antiquities and fortune hunting. This particular person proved to be a slippery fish and evaded any serious charges.

As Sarah stared out the rainy window, her thoughts drifted back to the previous year when she and her sister wandered in the woods and she wondered where her life was going. She was so thankful for the improvement in her health and to have a life partner that was her real treasure.

She always loved a mystery and anything outdoors, but how was she to know that it would all combine and turn into something beautiful?

It was the blueberries that started it all, but actually it was something deeper. Something rooted in the distant past that finally had come to pass.

It was going to be a another typical moody day along the Southern Coast as the fog rolled in among the sprawling oaks, and the Spanish moss wavered to and fro in the gentle morning breeze. How endearing was the sound of the loon as it echoed across the marshes and in amongst the trees.

www.ingramcontent.com/pod-product-compliance
Lightning Source LLC
Chambersburg PA
CBHW020406150626
46554CB00012B/394